He's your boss, your boss, your boss, *Lara repeated to herself.*

Derek's deep-set, hazel eyes narrowed with concern. They were filled with immeasurable warmth as he asked, "Are you okay?"

"Yes, I'm fine." *The world is spinning, and I'm getting older. And all I can think about is how sexy you look.*

"Do you need anything?"

She shook her head, thinking she might tell him how she ached to hold her own baby someday. "Are you here with your son?" she asked, straining for a smile. He'd make beautiful babies, she decided.

"Joey and I came to the park to play catch. And for his favorite, hot dogs."

"That's a favorite of mine, too." Lara stood up to leave. "Well, I'll see you back at the office." She swung away, smiling. With excruciating honesty, she admitted how difficult it was to ignore the emotions he stirred within her.

"Lara?"

In midstride, she paused and shot a look over her shoulder at him.

His long, hard look nearly melted her bones. "You look terrific."

Breathe, Lara, breathe. "Thank you."

Dear Reader,

We're delighted to feature Jennifer Mikels, who penned the second story in our multiple-baby-focused series, MANHATTAN MULTIPLES. Jennifer writes, "To me, there's something wonderfully romantic about a doctor-nurse story and about a crush developing into a forever love. In *The Fertility Factor* (#1559), a woman's love touches a man's heart and teaches him that what he thought was impossible is within his reach if he'll trust her enough."

Sherryl Woods continues to captivate us with *Daniel's Desire* (#1555), the conclusion of her celebrated miniseries THE DEVANEYS. When a runaway girl crosses their paths, a hero and heroine reunite despite their tragic past. And don't miss *Prince and Future...Dad?* (#1556), the second book in Christine Rimmer's exciting miniseries VIKING BRIDES, in which a princess experiences a night of passion and gets the surprise of a lifetime! *Quinn's Woman* (#1557), by Susan Mallery is the next in her longtime-favorite HOMETOWN HEARTBREAKERS miniseries. Here, a self-defense expert never expects to find hand-to-heart combat with her rugged instructor....

Return to the latest branch of popular miniseries MONTANA MAVERICKS: THE KINGSLEYS with *Marry Me...Again* (#1558) by Cheryl St.John. This dramatic tale shows a married couple experiencing some emotional bumps—namely that their marriage is invalid! Will they break all ties or rediscover a love that's always been there? Then, *Found in Lost Valley* (#1560) by Laurie Paige, the fourth title in her SEVEN DEVILS miniseries, is about two people with secrets in their pasts, but who can't deny the rising tensions between them!

As you can see, we have a lively batch of stories, delivering diversity and emotion in each romance.

Happy reading!

Sincerely,

Karen Taylor Richman
Senior Editor

Please address questions and book requests to:
Silhouette Reader Service
U.S.: 3010 Walden Ave., P.O. Box 1325, Buffalo, NY 14269
Canadian: P.O. Box 609, Fort Erie, Ont. L2A 5X3

The Fertility Factor

JENNIFER MIKELS

Silhouette®

SPECIAL EDITION™

Published by Silhouette Books

America's Publisher of Contemporary Romance

Special thanks and acknowledgment are given to
Jennifer Mikels for her contribution
to the MANHATTAN MULTIPLES series.

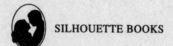 SILHOUETTE BOOKS

ISBN 0-373-24559-9

THE FERTILITY FACTOR

Books by Jennifer Mikels

Silhouette Special Edition

A Sporting Affair #66
Whirlwind #124
Remember the Daffodils #478
Double Identity #521
Stargazer #574
Freedom's Just Another Word #623
A Real Charmer #694
A Job for Jack #735
Your Child, My Child #807
Denver's Lady #870
Jake Ryker's Back in Town #929
Sara's Father #947
Child of Mine #993
Expecting: Baby #1023
Married...with Twins! #1054
Remember Me? #1107
A Daddy for Devin #1150
The Marriage Bargain #1168
Temporary Daddy #1192
Just the Three of Us #1251
Forever Mine #1265
The Bridal Quest #1360
The Child She Always Wanted #1410
Her Hand-Picked Family #1415
Big Sky Cowboy #1491
The Fertility Factor #1559

Silhouette Romance

Lady of the West #462
Maverick #487
Perfect Partners #511
The Bewitching Hour #551

JENNIFER MIKELS

is from Chicago, Illinois, but resides now in Phoenix, Arizona, with her husband, two sons and a shepherd-collie. She enjoys reading, sports, antiques, yard sales and long walks. Though she's done technical writing in public relations, she loves writing romances and happy endings.

MANHATTAN MULTIPLES

So much excitement happening at once!

The doors of Manhattan Multiples might close.
The mayor and Eloise Vale once had a thing.
Someone on the staff is pregnant
and is keeping it a secret.
Romance and drama—
and so many babies in the big city!

Dr. Derek Cross—Best-looking single-dad doctor in the city, or at least that's what Lara Mancini thinks. But with a painful divorce under his belt and his busy life, will Derek surrender to secret fantasies about his nurse?

Lara Mancini—Dr Cross's nurse is in love with her boss. And while Lara loves taking care of people, her biological clock is ticking. Will she and Derek find a way to stop time in its tracks?

Allison Baker—Assistant to Manhattan Multiples' director, this shy beauty is about to let loose for the first time in her life. And when she does, one Prince Charming will find her irresistible and will go to the ends of the earth to find his runaway princess.

A man walks into a bar...and meets the woman of his dreams. Can a firefighting hero and a vivacious free-spirit pull off the performance of a lifetime without falling in love? Find out in next month's HIS PRETEND FIANCÉE, by Victoria Pade (SE #1564).

Prologue

"Daddy, I'm talking about a girlfriend."

Derek Cross set a hand on his five-year-old son's shoulder and slowed their pace to weave a path around pigeons pecking at the cement. "You have a girlfriend?" he asked while he urged his son into Central Park.

Head back, Joey squinched his nose. "Not me."

He'd thought his son was still in his I-don't-like-girls stage. "So who has one?"

"No one does."

Where was this conversation going? Derek wondered. Through sunglasses, he squinted up at the clear blue sky and bright summer sun. Usually he had no trouble following his son's disorganized conversations. "Joey, let's start over."

"Can I have an ice cream?" Joey asked, pointing in the direction of a vendor.

Derek ran a hand over the top of Joey's shiny, dark-brown hair, then plopped the baseball cap back on the boy's head. "After lunch."

"If we have lunch, will we get home in time?"

"In time for what?" What was his concern this time? At five, Joey fretted with the expertise of a forty-year-old. "Mommy doesn't come for you today," Derek reminded him.

"The ball game, Daddy. You said you'd have time to watch it with me."

"Some of it. Joey, about what you were saying. Who has a girlfriend?"

Imitating a professional ballplayer's actions, Joey slapped the baseball into his mitt. "You need one."

"I—" The last time he'd been speechless had been the day Joey was born. "I...need one?"

"Uh-huh. Someone special."

Derek managed not to laugh. "Why do I?"

"Because you're lonely."

That was news to him. *Busy* described his life better. Between his medical practice and his son, he hadn't had time to bother with more than casual dating. But even if he had more time, after his marriage had failed, he'd vowed never again. Love was the last thing he wanted. "Who said I am?" Derek asked, certain someone had put the idea in Joey's head.

"Mommy says so."

He should have known. Leave it to Rose. Despite the divorce three years ago—because he and Rose had parted amicably, she never hesitated to voice her opinion about his love life or, in her words, "lack of it."

"Mommy's going on a date," Joey added.

Derek had heard, wished her well. But he understood now what was happening. Rose figured if she was dating, it was time for him, too. They needed to talk. "What else did Mommy say?"

"She said she's going on a vacation before she clapses."

Derek chuckled. "Before she clapses."

"That's what she said."

"I believe you, Joey." He checked his watch, promised himself he wouldn't do that again while with Joey, but mentally he calculated time. With luck, before he had to leave for appointments, he'd manage to watch two innings of the ball game with his son.

"Mommy said you need a date."

Was he really having a conversation about his lack of female companions with his five-year-old son? You need a life, Doc, he mused. "Come on. Let's play ball."

"Do you know a girl, Daddy?"

Plenty of them. But if he could pick and choose, he already had a candidate, his nurse. A tall, willowy knockout with a flawless, fair complexion, long blond hair and green eyes. "I know some, Joey." Like Lara Mancini with the bright, pearly white smile and delicate features. "Don't worry about me."

Chapter One

"You're such a natural with them, Lara."

Lara Mancini cradled the six-week-old girl in her arms and smiled. "I've had a lot of practice. Last count, I had ten nieces and nephews."

Standing beside her, the beaming mom and dad of the triplets each held one infant.

In the three years since Lara had volunteered as a nurse at Manhattan Multiples, a center for multiple births, she'd held many babies, but she never lost interest or felt too tired to hold one. While still in her teens and baby-sitting for every neighbor on the block, she realized how much she loved being with children.

"You should be a mother, Lara," the woman said.

"Someday. Your next appointment is in six months

unless you need to see Dr. Cross sooner,'' Lara said
while placing the little one in an infant seat.

"No, I'm feeling great.'' The young woman shot
a meaningful look at her husband as they bent down
to place the other two babies in car seats.

Lara assumed the silent exchange carried a definite
message of intimacy since they'd received the all-
clear to resume relations.

"Come on,'' her husband urged. "Lara has other
patients to care for.''

"I always enjoy being with these three,'' Lara assured them. She smiled, watched them leave. The
daddy carted out two infant seats, while his wife managed one and an oversize pink-and-blue diaper bag.
Lara cast a look at the gallery clock on the half wall
behind the appointment counter. The appointments on
this Saturday morning had been lighter than usual.

Having promised to meet co-workers downstairs in
the reception area a few minutes before noon, she
hurried into the staff lounge, and rushed to her locker
to change out of blue-colored scrubs. She slid on a
deep-green, V-necked, sleeveless top and an ankle-
length, silk floral skirt, released her hair from the tor-
toiseshell clasp and fluffed it. After snatching up her
shoulder bag from her locker, she dashed to the elevator.

On the way down to the first floor, she attached
small, gold hoop earrings and a gold chain to dress
up the outfit. She thought about what the couple had
said to her. Everyone said the same. She was a natural
with babies.

You should be a mother. Her stomach knotted. She wasn't one, might never be. Depressing thoughts had started at seven that morning. Over the phone a friend, fighting tears, had told her terrible news. Sadness had shadowed Lara ever since Gena's call about her appointment at her gynecologist.

As the elevator doors swooshed open, Lara fought her sad mood. In the lobby she saw Eloise Vale, Manhattan Multiples' director disappear into her office. Another nurse, Carrie Williamson, was waiting beside Josie Tate's desk.

The center's receptionist, Josie, was a cute, petite brunette with an abundance of blond streaks, who favored denim clothes. Her bright smile was the first thing people saw when they entered Manhattan Multiples.

"I'm sorry I'm late," Lara said to both of them from a few feet away.

"No problem." Carrie, a tall brunette with a slight build, led the way to the center's entrance. "I've been telling Josie about my latest dating fiasco," she said while pushing open one of the double glass doors. A man bumped shoulders with Carrie, as he plowed his way through the crowd. "I'm looking for a prince among frogs."

Lara knew where there was one—Dr. Derek Cross. Handsome, rich, charming. She kept the thought to herself. Never had he indicated interest in her, but from day one, she'd felt a tightness in her chest whenever he was near. Her secret crush was her business, no one else's. She liked her job, wanted to keep it.

"I can't believe how hot it is," Josie said.

"Neither can I," Lara agreed when they stopped at a curb for a red light. A summer heat wave for the past two days had left New Yorkers cranky.

"That's a great outfit, Lara."

Josie nodded her agreement of Carrie's comment.

"Thanks. I didn't think scrubs would play well today." For the upscale restaurant near the center's Madison Avenue address, she and Carrie had changed outfits.

It was their splurge week. Instead of the deli nearby, the three women strolled to a pricey restaurant with rosewood paneled walls, crystal, linen and enormous flower arrangements. Inside, the buzz of conversation and the clink of silverware filled the room.

Even after they were seated at a table for four, Carrie continued to rattle on about her date two nights ago. "He bought me a hot dog. That was his idea of a big date. Then we took a taxi to the theater. He was out of money. I ask you. Why did he suggest the taxi if he couldn't pay for it? Because he knew he couldn't. How insulting."

Lara sipped her water and absently listened to Josie offering sympathetic words to Carrie about her tale of woe.

Josie poked a fork into the shrimp salad just delivered, but paused with the fork in midair. "Lara, are you sick? You're awfully quiet."

"I'm in trouble," Lara answered, frowning at her Caesar salad.

As if playing a child's game of Red Light, Green Light, they both froze.

"You're pregnant?" Carrie mumbled, her mouth full.

"You would have told us if you were, wouldn't you?" Josie asked.

"I'm not pregnant," Lara said, "and that's what's really wrong. Time is running out for me."

"To get pregnant, you mean?" Josie asked.

Lara nodded. "I used to believe that I had plenty of time to think about a husband, about tying myself down, about children. But I'm thirty-eight. I feel pressure now to get pregnant soon, before it's too late."

Carrie shook her head. "Oh, you'll be okay."

Did they really understand? Lara wondered. Carrie perhaps did. She was thirty-two and divorced. But Josie might not understand her desperation. Often Josie had scoffed at the idea of having children. But then Josie was only twenty-five. She could afford to be a free spirit for a few more years.

"Anyone would want you," Carrie said.

Lara laughed. How sweet she was. "No, they wouldn't. Men my age want sexy young things with thighs of steel."

"You have thighs of steel."

Lara nearly snorted. "They're not Jell-O—well, maybe firm Jell-O."

"I've seen you in a bikini," Josie cut in. "Most women would die for your figure, Lara. You're pretty enough to be a movie star."

"She was a movie star," Carrie reminded her.

Lara had strived for a long time to earn her living doing something she loved—acting. But like others with "pie in the sky" dreams, she'd faced the truth several years ago. Though she'd known a more glamorous life, had acted in a Broadway play, even a few movies, she doubted she'd make it big as an actress.

"I don't know how you could give all that up," Carrie said.

"It wasn't that glamorous. Where are you performing this week, Josie?"

"Goodfellows." At night Josie hung out at coffee shops or smoky bars where she read her poetry. "It's an upscale bar in the West Village. Will you come? It's not far from your place."

"I'll try." Lara had saved diligently and had invested well to afford a one-bedroom apartment in the West Village building, complete with a doorman.

"Me, too," Carrie said between bites of her chicken sandwich.

They stayed longer than they should have and rushed back toward the center at Madison Avenue and Seventy-eighth Street. Lara said goodbye as the other women were about to enter the center, said she had an errand to run. She had time before the first afternoon appointment arrived. The truth was she wanted to be alone. She needed time to think.

She wandered into Central Park, found a bench. She'd been deadly serious with her co-workers. Her usual optimism had waned with her friend Gena's early-morning, tearful phone call. Lara had ached for her. The news had stormed her with doubts and despair about her own ability to get pregnant.

In two years she'd celebrate her fortieth birthday. She didn't have time anymore. She needed to get pregnant now.

"It's lunchtime, Mancini. What are you doing sitting here, alone?"

The male voice jerked her head up. Even with sunlight in her eyes, she knew who stood before her. Light glowed around him, but she saw the easy, half smile tugging at a corner of his lips.

"Hi." Mentally she prodded herself to act normal. That was no easy task. Derek Cross tripped every feminine instinct within her. "The park's a good place to think." He's your boss, your boss, your boss, Lara repeated to herself like a mantra.

Beneath dark, straight brows, his deep-set, hazel eyes narrowed with concern. She ranked his eyes as one of his best features. Cool, unreadable—sometimes. Filled with unmeasurable warmth during other moments, like today. "Are you okay?"

The light breeze tossed his dark-brown hair. She thought he was even sexier with the strands slightly disturbed, mussed in much the way they'd look from a woman's touch. "Yes, I'm fine." The world is spinning, and I'm getting older. And all I can think about is how sexy you look. The black polo shirt clung to muscled biceps and a lean, flat belly. She'd just known he would have such a well-toned body. Denim curved around a tight butt and followed long, strong-looking legs. A shiver inched its way up her spine.

She wouldn't drool, she promised herself. It didn't matter that she was much too old for such nonsense. He made her hot, all six-four of him. "Have you had your lunch yet?"

He tipped his head slightly in a questioning manner.

Mentally she moaned. Did he think she was asking him to have lunch with her? "I mean—" Oh, this was insane. She was an intelligent woman who managed to snag even a stranger's attention with interesting conversation, so why was she acting like a ninny? "I just finished having it. My lunch." Scintillating, Lara. This will undoubtedly be the last time he talked to her about anything except a patient. At the office he'd always been all business. "With Josie and Carrie." She needed to get a grip. "Do you know them?"

His eyes held an amused smile. "Yes, I know them."

"I—" She paused, vowed to drown herself if she blushed. She needed to pretend they were at work. Tongue-tied was not normal for her. If anything, she'd been accused, mainly by family, of being gabby.

"Do you need anything?"

Oh, what a question.

"Is there something I can do to help? If there is, tell me," Derek added while he braced the bicycle he'd ridden to the park against the bench.

She shook her head, wished he'd stop asking. She might tell him that she was frightened. She wanted to hold a baby. She ached to hold her own baby. "Are you here with your son?" she asked, and strained for a smile. He'd make beautiful babies, she decided. The boys would have that long, straight nose, that strong, sharply angled face. They'd be as gorgeous as their father.

"Joey and I came to the park to play catch."

From previous conversations with him, she knew that he and his son usually went to the park on the weekends. As Derek shifted his stance, she realized he'd angled his body while talking to her so he never lost sight of his son. She thought the boy with his dark-brown hair and blue eyes already had his father's great looks.

"And we came for lunch. One of my son's favorites. Hot dogs."

Lara stood up to leave. "That's a favorite of mine, too," she said but didn't move as he smiled. She liked his mouth, too. Firm looking with a full bottom lip. Then there were the slashing high cheekbones. She'd always been a sucker for a man with high cheekbones.

"I've heard you're a fantastic cook. I wouldn't think you'd touch a hot dog."

She barely kept an idiotic grin from forming. What a perfect opportunity to say she'd be glad to cook him something some evening. Of course, she couldn't. "I like cooking. Even hot dogs."

"Anyone who can cook hot dogs rates high with my son. Is today special?" he asked, gesturing toward her clothes.

"We—" She paused. During her stint as an actress, she'd kissed a few heart-stopping, handsome males. Didn't matter. She was sunk around Derek Cross. "We had an expensive lunch today—a once-a-month treat."

"Nice."

Dumbly she waited for him to say more.

Instead he shot a look at his son and beckoned him toward them. "Do you remember Ms. Mancini, Joey?"

"My name's Lara." She'd met him a few times before when Derek had brought him to the office, but he'd been younger, and she assumed he wouldn't remember her. She gestured toward Joey's baseball mitt. "Your dad told me that you love baseball."

Derek frowned. "Did I?"

A twinge of disappointment whipped through her. She'd been so thrilled when he'd shared his celebratory mood and had told her about his son's first home run on the previous day. "Yes, in passing."

"I remember you. Do you want to play?" Joey asked.

Derek touched his slender shoulder. "Joey, she can't—"

"I could, if I had more time. I love baseball, too." Lara glanced at her watch, a serviceable round face with a black band. "Do you like the Yankees?"

"Yeah!"

"Me, too. I try never to miss a game."

"There's one on television today."

"I know," Lara said. "But I can't watch it. I have

to get back to work." Maybe she was talking too much.

Derek sent her a questioning look. "I'd never have guessed you were a fan. Baseball seems too quiet for you."

A laugh bubbled in her throat. "Too quiet?" Amusement stayed with her. She knew his background. The Cross family claimed a lineage that dated back to the American Colonies. How did Derek view her? Flighty? Eccentric? Because she'd been an actress? She'd learned from one man that the upper crust viewed theater people as a step above bohemians. James Braden III had made it clear that greasepaint and blue blood didn't mix. "I have brothers. Quiet is not in the Mancini vocabulary."

Derek flashed a smile. "They play ball?"

"One of them was always asking me to play catch."

"I gather you come from a big family?"

"Three brothers, two sisters," she said, feeling more at ease because Joey was near.

"I never knew that about you."

Why would he? She was his nurse, nothing more. He'd have no reason to bother finding out anything about her. But he knew about her love of cooking? Why? Had he asked about her? Probably not, she decided. Someone might have said something, maybe at Christmastime when they'd had a potluck buffet at the center and everyone had brought a homemade dish. "Maybe some other time we can play," she said, just to please the boy. She knew she'd never be with them again. "If that's all right with your daddy," she added.

Joey sent her a quick grin, obviously taking her words to heart. "Is it, Dad?"

With a gentle hand, Derek cupped his son's shoulder. "We'll see."

A nice, noncommittal response, Lara mused.

"Daddy, can we go now?"

"I promised we'd watch the ball game until I have to leave," Derek said to her.

During the three years since she'd begun working side by side with Derek, Lara had never seen him look so relaxed. It had nothing to do with the clothes. It was the way he looked at his son. No strain tightened his jawline. No annoyance narrowed his eyes. He looked so calm.

Joey took a step away, then halted, remembering her. "Bye, Lara."

"See you, Joey." She waited until he was out of hearing range. "He's so adorable, Derek."

"I think so. That was nice of you," he said. "I owe you."

She swung away, smiling. With excruciating honesty, she admitted her feelings for this man were like a teenage crush. That sounded incredibly immature for a thirty-eight-year-old woman, but she couldn't ignore the emotions he stirred.

"Lara?"

In midstride, she paused, shot a look over her shoulder at him. She'd thought they were done.

His long, hard look nearly melted her bones. "You look terrific."

Breathe, Lara, breathe. "Thank you." During sensible moments she told herself that he'd probably drive her crazy with his inflexibility. She was a "wing it" person. Five siblings had forced her to have an easygoing nature. Adaptability was a must with a capital *A*. Derek definitely was intense, all wrong for her. He was also out of her league. But it didn't matter a whit that they had nothing in common except a love for kids. She had the hots for him.

Derek watched her walk away and swore softly. She hadn't told him what was wrong. He'd seen her sitting on the park bench. Head bent, she'd looked so alone. He'd never seen her alone. People gravitated toward her. At work someone—a patient's family or a co-worker—was always talking to her.

"She's pretty."

Derek caught his son's small hand and grabbed the handlebar of the bicycle. "Yes."

More than one nurse had complained that he was aloof, detached, distant. He'd gone through several nurses before Lara had worked for him. He was too much of a perfectionist, people claimed. He expected too much, was tough on the people who worked with him. He didn't think so. Babies, precious and innocent, were in his care. They deserved the best he and everyone he worked with could give them. He'd found that person when Lara Mancini had come to work with him. He'd be a fool to ruin the working relationship he had with her.

"She likes you. I can tell."

Derek chuckled. "How can you tell?" he asked, interested in hearing his son's observation.

"Because she smiled at you a lot. A real lot. Rylyn liked Adam and smiled at him all the time."

"Who's Rylyn?"

"The one with the pink lunch box at school."

"Oh, okay." Rylyn, a kindergarten classmate, was a dimpled redhead with freckles.

"When they like you, they smile a lot."

Derek grinned. Was he really getting advice from his five-year-old son?

"And you smiled at her a lot, too."

"We work together, Joey. Lara is my nurse."

"Couldn't she be your girlfriend?"

"I don't think so." No, she couldn't. He knew she couldn't be. Lara Mancini wanted everything he was rejecting—promises, commitment, love, marriage and children. Derek tightened his hand on his son's. Joey had gone through everything that Derek had promised himself no child of his ever would. He'd never do that to another child.

"Daddy, you're doing it again."

"Doing what?"

"I'm talking to you, and you're not listening." Joey frowned. "In school, you get your name on the board if you do that."

Derek pulled a silly face and whacked the side of his head. "Me? I did that. *Again?*" As Joey laughed at him, Derek dropped to his haunches. "Climb aboard."

Joey placed one arm around Derek's neck and gripped his shirt at the shoulder with his other hand. "Couldn't she be?" he asked, straddling Derek's back for a piggyback ride.

Derek paused in walking the bike and unhooked the water bottle from behind the seat to offer Joey a drink.

"I was thirsty." He gulped a mouthful of water, then handed Derek the water bottle.

"Joey, what is this about?" Derek asked and took a hearty swallow of the water.

"You have to like her to make a baby, don't you?"

The water spewed out of his mouth. "What? Who said anything about babies?" He'd have a long talk with his ex-wife if she was putting this stuff in Joey's head.

"Rylyn said I need to be a big brother. Everyone in my class is having a baby."

Rylyn again. "They are?"

"Even the turtle. They lay eggs. Mrs. Wolken has a big egg in her."

Mrs. Wolken was a kindergarten teacher in her last trimester. "She doesn't have an egg in her. She has a baby."

"Uh-huh. A baby is inside an egg."

They'd talk tonight at bedtime. Now wasn't the time to have a discussion about the birds and bees. "Let's get home. Dorothy is making your favorite cookies," he said about Dorothy Donaldson, housekeeper, nanny, good friend. She wore a lot of hats for them. "She's waiting for you to help."

Joey leaned close and whispered in his ear. "Chocolate chip?"

"Aren't they your favorite?"

"Uh-huh." He hugged Derek's neck tighter. "I like Lara," he added.

So did he. She revved his motor, especially today in that outfit. Possibly he was thinking so much about her because she'd looked different today. Classy. Sexy.

Chapter Two

Even when Lara was in an annoyed mood, Manhattan Multiple's warm blue interior calmed her. Hot from her walk to the center, she welcomed the coolness in the air-conditioned center's reception area.

Josie sat on a chair behind the front desk. At Lara's entrance, she signaled to her. "I wanted to tell you more at lunch," she whispered. "But I didn't want to say anything in front of Carrie and be a source of gossip." She looked up as a middle-aged woman with salt-and-pepper hair passed by.

Along with Josie, Lara said hello.

"A new doctor. A perinatologist, like Dr. Cross." Josie glanced away to smile when another employee, Allison Baker, also passed by them. In her mid-twenties, she was thin, with chin-length auburn-colored hair. Lara thought of her as rather sweet, maybe a touch too prim. Josie, who stood several inches shorter than Allison, had become a good friend of hers in a short amount of time. "She's in love," Josie said.

Lara smiled. "She told you?"

"No, you can tell," Josie said, nodding her head. Overhead lights highlighted the blond streaks threaded through brown strands. "She met someone last month. That's what you need."

"What do I need?" Lara asked.

"A handsome stranger."

Lara knew a man who suited her just fine. "Is that what you wanted to talk about?"

"No." Josie hunched forward. "Eloise received e-mail from the mayor. She was really upset. I mean *really.*"

Lara assumed Josie heard that from Allison Baker, Eloise's personal assistant.

"No one knows what he wrote, but Eloise is usually so calm and sweet. Whatever he said disturbed her."

Mentally Lara shook her head. She found it hard to believe that Mayor Bill Harper was going out of his way to make Eloise's life miserable. Lara liked the mayor, believed he was an honest, straightforward man.

"Interesting, isn't it?" Josie asked.

"Could be." Lara refrained from saying more when she didn't know all the facts. "I'll talk to you later."

Getting time to do anything became an impossibil-
ity. Busy all day, Lara ushered one of the last patients
of the day to the door. "Won't be long now," she
said to the woman, who carried a burden that made
her every step slow and labored. But the woman was
fortunate. For someone carrying multiple babies,
she'd had a relatively normal pregnancy—no morning
sickness, no gestation diabetes.

The woman released a short laugh. "I'm looking
forward to seeing my feet. I suppose everyone says
that."

Lara nodded. Most pregnant women made a similar
complaint. She would love to have the problem. If
she ever got pregnant, she'd relish every single moment, including the ones that made her feel lousy.
Because she was still troubled about Gena's news,
she'd struggled with smiles all day. Though she had
a dozen things to do after work, including laundry,
she decided to relax with a book and a glass of wine
after she got home.

The workday stretched longer than she'd expected.
Everyone had left long ago, and she was still there.
So was Derek. The woman in the examining room
had complained about heavy discharge since her
babies' birth. An erosion of the cervix, an occasional
problem following delivery, had required an in-office
procedure. Derek had cauterized the cervical area
with no discomfort to the woman. While the patient
dressed to leave, Lara enjoyed spending the time with
the woman's twins.

"They're staying even." Lara commented to the

woman when she emerged from the examining room to leave.

"They've both gained another pound. Devin is a half inch bigger than Ian."

"He's the oldest, isn't he?" Lara said.

"Born one minute and fifty-five seconds before his brother."

"He'll probably never let him forget that," Derek said, coming up behind them in the outer office.

"I expect that's true," the mother said.

"You're going on vacation, aren't you?" Lara asked her as Derek left them to return to his office.

"Yes." She checked on her babies in the blue-plaid baby carriage. "It's a family holiday at Martha's Vineyard. Dr. Cross said he vacationed there as a child."

"I'm sure it's nice."

And a place for the affluent. Unlike his family, hers originally resided in New York's Little Italy.

Lara saw the woman out to the waiting room, then wandered into the staff lounge. It was late. She knew security had escorted the woman and her babies to a taxi. Thunder rumbled angrily and lightning flashed, casting the offices in an eerie glow.

Uneasy about the lateness more than the weather, she moved quickly. With another flash of lightning, she hurried to her locker and snatched up her umbrella, then grabbed her shoulder bag. Her footsteps echoed on the floor before she hit the carpeted hallway. From a distance, she heard the elevator doors open and ran the rest of the way. A few lab techni-

cians were still in the building. She'd rather ride down
with them than be alone. Nearing the elevator, she
saw the doors stood open, waiting for her.

Just inside, Derek grinned. "Want to ride down
together?"

Winded, her heart pounding, Lara pressed a hand
to her chest. "Yes." She stood only inches from him.
With his lengthy look, she struggled for conversation.
"I always liked storms." Since coming in this morning, neither of them had said anything about their
meeting in the park. She'd felt closer to him there.
But except for this brief conversation, they were back
to all business. Of course, they'd been busy all day.
But he'd acted as if those moments had never happened.

Nervous in the quiet elevator with him, she went
into her survival mode. She talked. Talked about the
patients, about lunch at the exquisite restaurant, about
his son. "He's really cute, Dr. Cross."

"Lara, away from the office, don't you think you
should call me Derek?"

Okeydokey. "Derek." She took a deep breath.
"Wasn't there a doctors' staff meeting this morning?
Have you heard more about the feud between Eloise
and the mayor?" She wondered if he knew more than
the rest of the staff about the situation between Eloise
and the mayor. "Do you think Manhattan Multiples
might close?"

"If Bill Harper is serious about stopping funding,
that could happen."

Lara frowned. "Some of the staff are concerned they might lose their jobs."

"You shouldn't worry. You're an excellent nurse. You'd never have a problem finding a new job."

He looked down at his watch, frowned. He had somewhere to go, someone waiting for him. She wasn't surprised. He was considered quite a catch by co-workers. Because she was taken with him, Lara always kept her thoughts about him to herself, not wanting to reveal the crush she had on him.

"I'm going to be in trouble tonight."

Someone special was waiting for him. I don't want to hear this, she thought.

"I promised to cook sloppy joes."

"You eat sloppy joe sandwiches?" she asked about the messy hamburger mix on a bun. She couldn't visualize a butler serving that.

He laughed. "I brush my teeth, too."

She felt heat sweep over her face.

"I'm sorry." He flashed a smile that nearly buckled her knees. "I couldn't resist teasing."

"I'm just surprised that you cook." Especially something appropriate for eating on a TV tray. The man came from money. Wasn't he accustomed to servants?

"Only sloppy joes. Dorothy cooks the rest of our meals. You know who I mean. You've talked to her."

"Yes." She'd had brief conversations with his housekeeper-nanny. While he withdrew his cell phone, she stepped back to give him privacy, but it wasn't difficult to hear.

"Dorothy, I'm leaving now and—what the…" The elevator jerked, then stopped. He caught Lara's wrist to steady her. "Are you okay?"

Sensation stirred deep within her. He had to be kidding? He was touching her. She couldn't think about anything else.

"Dorothy, I'm going to be a little late, I think." Repeatedly he pushed at the alarm button. Nothing happened. "Damn. No medical emergency…." he explained to Dorothy. "A sick elevator. It stalled. I'll call you back."

As he swung a look at Lara, she gave him a faint smile. She was stuck in an elevator with him. They could be there for hours. Overnight. What should she talk about? Maybe she shouldn't say anything. Lord, she didn't want to act like a ninny.

"Are you claustrophobic?"

No, that wasn't her problem. "No."

He grinned at her. "Fearless, aren't you?"

Lara wasn't sure what he meant.

"You like storms, don't panic being stuck in an elevator. Fearless."

"I don't think about where we are. Being stuck in an elevator between floors could be unnerving, but it won't be if you don't think about it." How simple she made that sound, how calm she appeared. Far from it. She drew a deep breath. It was insane to be so uneasy. She talked to him every day. So what if they were in a closet-size space? So what if there was no one around to act as a buffer?

"You did a good job with Mrs. Benson. She was

stressing until you reassured her. I'm glad you were here for her this evening. You seem to know the right thing to say," Derek said.

Business. Okay, that would be best. They'd discuss business. "Thank you."

He gave her a look of compassion. "Lara, could you use a sympathetic shoulder?"

"Why would you think that?" She hadn't thought anyone had noticed her blue mood, especially him.

He stared long and hard at her as if trying to see inside her. "You didn't bubble today."

"Bubble?" He thought she bubbled? Her laugh slipped out.

"You usually bubble. You're the sunniest, most smiley person I've ever met. But you looked as if you were working at those smiles today."

Deliberately she feigned a bright one.

"It's not working."

Lara heard the teasing lilt in his voice and found herself smiling. "It's not?"

"No. You said that you're not worried about the center closing. Do you have a different work problem?"

"No, I don't." She hesitated then realized she could have talked to co-workers about this at lunch. Why hadn't she? Why did she feel like sharing her heartache for a friend with him? "I received a call from a high-school friend this morning and—" Her words remained unfinished as the elevator moved a few inches, then jerked to a stop again.

"Hello," a male voice yelled down to them. "Anyone there?"

"Yeah, Frank," Derek called back.

Lara was touched that he knew the name of the building's security man, a retired police detective.

"It's Derek Cross and Lara Mancini."

Lara mentally groaned. The gossips would have fun tomorrow with that news. She could imagine the whispered words. Guess who was stuck in the elevator? Alone. For hours.

"Dr. Cross, I'll get maintenance right on it," Frank yelled. "You two will be out in a jiffy."

"Thanks, Frank," Derek called back. Swinging a look at her, he shrugged. "We're stuck. He'll get maintenance—"

"Right on it," she finished for him. Now what? "Looks as if we'll have plenty of time."

"Finish telling me about your friend."

As long as she didn't think too much about them, about the excitement that tingled her skin whenever he was near, she'd make sense. "She's the same age as me." When Gena had called, panic had rushed through Lara. Gena's problem could easily be her own. "She has endometrioses."

"She's been to a specialist?"

"Yes. The doctor told Gena she might need a hysterectomy."

"No kids?" Derek asked, leaning against the back wall of the elevator.

"No, she doesn't have any. Learning about Gena

has made me aware that time is getting away from me.''

''You have time.''

''Not really.'' If he'd kiss her, just once, maybe she'd stop thinking about it. ''I'm thirty-eight.''

''I assume you mean the biological clock is ticking.''

Lara nodded. ''Having children matters to me. A lot. I can't wait any longer.''

''I didn't know there was someone special in your life.''

This wasn't something she wanted to admit to him. ''There isn't.''

''Are you talking about artificial—''

Oh, this was too much. Embarrassing. She sounded as if she was a charity case, couldn't attract a man. ''No, no,'' Lara cut in. ''I won't do that. But I've made a decision.'' She might as well level with him, tell him what he'd probably learn via the center's gossip grapevine. ''Within the next six months, I'll make every effort to find Mr. Right, to get married. So within the year, I'll get pregnant.''

''You make that sound easy.''

She nearly laughed. ''It isn't or I wouldn't be in this predicament.''

''You'll forget about love and orange blossoms and whatever else?'' He smiled again. She realized she loved the way his lips curved in a slow-forming smile. ''Are you thinking about a sperm bank?''

Lara rolled her eyes at him. ''I can't go to a sperm bank or do in-vitro fertilization.''

"Can't or won't?"

"Won't. I come from an Italian-American family that believes motherhood is sacred. They'd never understand if I had a baby any way but by the traditional way."

"So you're looking for—"

Why had she revealed so much to him? "Mr. Right," she finished for him. "You sound skeptical. Don't you believe there is a Mr. Right?"

"Could be fantasy."

"You're a skeptic about love?"

"For me." He frowned as if he was surprised he'd told her that. "No man is perfect, Lara."

"No, but someone could be perfect for me."

He arched a brow. "I guess that's realistic. What will you do? Look for someone you have a lot in common with?"

"That would probably be best. I have a few annoying traits."

The tease was in his eyes again. "You do?"

"My family claims I talk too much." He probably thought so, too. But she rambled when nervous or excited.

"But you're interesting."

Interesting. Her pulse thudded. "And I laugh a lot."

"Cheerful."

To say she wasn't pleased by his take on her would have been a blatant lie. "I drive some people crazy because it takes me a while to finish jobs. I have good intentions, but no one ever said you couldn't enjoy yourself while doing chores. Right?''

He shrugged. ''I'm from the do-it-and-get-it-done school.''

He wouldn't understand. Someone like him would think she was silly.

''What do you mean when you say it takes you a while? Why does it?''

She had no choice now except to be honest with him. ''I like to sing and dance. What my family will never let me live down is the time I was in the kitchen singing 'What's Love Got To Do with It,' while I was supposed to be drying dishes.''

Puzzlement veed his brows.

''I was standing on a kitchen chair with a turkey baster in my hand.''

''A turkey baster?''

''It was my microphone.''

He laughed, a deep rumbling laugh.

Enjoying herself, she went on, ''Since then, the running joke in my family is—expect Lara to take an hour to do a ten-minute task.''

''Love them, don't you?''

Was she imagining that he sounded envious? ''Immensely. And I know they love me. If they're enjoying themselves, I can be the brunt of their tease.''

''What kind of questions will you ask to find out if some guy is Mr. Right?''

''I…I never gave that a lot of thought. He'd have to be caring.'' She was a people person who'd take a walk on the weekend just to talk to neighbors. ''I suppose I'll ask what kind of music he likes. I like fifties and sixties hits the most, but will listen to almost any other kind of music. What do you listen to?''

"Classical. Opera.''

Lara nodded, not surprised. He probably went to the symphony before he was three. An exaggeration, she knew. But this man had led a life a world apart from hers. "I might ask my Mr. Right candidate what the last movie was that he saw.''

"That might not tell you anything about him.''

"Why not?''

He chuckled in private amusement. "Because the last movie I saw had a big mouse and raccoon in it.''

"Oh, I saw that, too. Cute, wasn't it?''

"I saw it because of my son. Why did you?''

With a turn of his head, the light overhead illuminated the strong lines of his face. She'd like to touch it, run her fingers over his cheek, his jaw. "Nieces and nephews,'' she answered.

"I guess it would be important for Mr. Right to like Italian food.''

He was perceptive. "I had it before baby formula.'' A man who didn't like Italian food would hate holidays with her family, any meal. Regardless of what was served, pork loin or ham or turkey, her mother always served a side of spaghetti or ravioli. And she would be insulted if the man didn't at least sample everything on her table. "I'd like it if he skied.''

"You ski?''

Lara shook her head. "I don't, but I'd like to.''

"So anyone who skis gets points?"

She laughed at how silly that sounded. "Yes, I guess so."

"What else?"

Was he, too, trying to keep conversation going? Never had they shared so much personal information with each other. "I like lazing around on days off, having breakfast in bed while I read the newspaper. Do you?"

"I get up at five to run in the park. Who serves you breakfast in bed?"

"No one." She knew what she was going to say would sound dumb. "I get up, make breakfast, bring it on a tray to the bed and pretend it was served. Sounds silly, huh?"

"No. You must have a great imagination."

Excitement stormed her as she watched his eyes briefly fall upon her lips. "I acted for a while."

"I know you did." He slid a hand into his slacks pocket. "Why the career change? Actress to nurse?"

"I had a calling." She assumed only another person in medicine would understand. "How far do you run?" She could probably manage a block or two.

"Three miles."

Lara mentally groaned at the thought of so much exercise. "Every morning?"

"Every morning."

He was disgustingly disciplined.

Looking down again, he gestured at the knitting needles sticking out of her shoulder bag. "What are you making?"

Feverishly she'd knit during every minute of her spare time. "It's an afghan. For a cousin's baby. Due in another month."

"A boy?" he asked, gesturing toward the blue yarn.

"Yes, he—" The elevator dropped. Two, maybe three inches. No more. Suddenly they stood in darkness. "Oh my God, Derek." She reached out, groped for him.

"I'm here." His hand caught hers and tugged her to him.

The back beneath her palms was solid, broad, muscular. Pulse pounding, she leaned away to see his face.

"Come on." He drew her even closer. "Sit on the floor with me. That would be smarter than standing."

He meant in case the elevator dropped, didn't he?

Despite his words, he wasn't moving, wasn't letting her go. She knew why. They stood breast to chest, thigh to thigh. Warmth radiated between them.

"It's nice," he said suddenly.

She thought the moment was wonderful. But possibly they weren't thinking about the same thing. "What is?"

"Your perfume. I never smelled it before."

He'd never been this close before. Every morning she dabbed a touch of perfume behind her ears to make her feel feminine while wearing scrubs. With the turn of his head, his breath heated her face. Even in the dark, she knew his mouth was closer to hers. Or was she imagining everything?

Lightly his lips brushed hers like a subtle caress.

Oh, Lord. She wasn't imagining anything. Her eyes fluttered, her lips parted for his. Slowly, almost savoringly he deepened the pressure. Gently his lips moved over hers. Wanting to feel more, she leaned closer, pressed her breasts into him to absorb the heat, the solidness of his body.

His kiss was everything she'd imagined. No. It was more. A long, pleasurable shiver swept through her. Eyes closed, she savored the sweet firmness of his mouth, the beat of his heart, the warmth of his body. With a kiss, he was making her feel more than she'd expected. In that instant, she knew this wouldn't be enough. She'd want more with him. Much more.

As she clung, he seemed to loosen his embrace. A touch dazed, she took a moment before she realized that he was pulling back. Why was he? Don't stop. *Keep kissing me.*

"Damn," he murmured in a voice that sounded huskier than usual.

Lara forced herself to open her eyes, heard his pager then. Kiss me again, she wanted to yell.

Chapter Three

Derek groped for the pager hooked on his belt and swore silently for a lot of reasons, including a need unfulfilled. One second more, and he'd have forgotten where they were.

Beneath the mantle of darkness, he peered at her face, at the hooded eyes, the soft mouth slightly parted. Her breath fluttered on his face and made him yearn for the sweetness of her mouth. Her scent stirred his senses. A heaviness still filled his loins.

In the dark he squinted to read the number on his pager. His emergency number meant Lindsey Collier was ready to deliver. She'd been admitted to the hospital yesterday for her safety and that of her quadruplets.

''The hospital?'' Lara asked.

"I've got to get out of here." Now. Urgency controlled him. He hated feeling so helpless about their situation. People claimed he was a control freak. He took no offense. In the operating room, he wanted to be in command. Lives depended on his leadership, skill and discipline.

"It's Lindsey Collier, isn't it?" Lara asked in the dark.

"Yes." It took effort to think clearly. Even now he touched her arm and visualized the creamy softness of her breasts.

"Dr. Cross!" Frank's voice sounded loud. Derek assumed he was crouched close to the elevator door. "Maintenance is here, working on the problem. Can you hear me?"

"I hear you. We need to get out now." He still felt the tug-of-war inside him. Emotional overload, he assured himself. "I have an emergency."

"A few minutes, Dr. Cross. We'll—" Frank stopped. No more words were needed. The light flashed on in the elevator. They heard a creak, a groan, then the elevator jerked and moved. Within seconds the doors swooshed open.

"Thanks, Frank." With a nod to the security man, he cupped a hand under Lara's elbow to urge her out of the elevator. A test of sorts to see if he could touch her casually.

"The storm knocked out power. We got everything running but the elevators. Sorry, Dr. Cross. We didn't know anyone was still in the building."

"No problem," Derek assured both men. Except

he almost made a move on his nurse, except she made him hungry. He knew about her crush. He'd have had to be dumb not to have noticed her unusual nervousness whenever they were alone. Only a jerk pursued a woman who wanted everything that he could never offer. "Lara, I have to get over to Lennox Hill."

"I'm going with you to the hospital," she said, falling in step with him toward the stairs.

Another nurse would have gone home. He liked her caring way that went beyond what was expected. "Lindsey Collier will like seeing you," he said honestly because her bright disposition would help. If he only lusted for her, he knew that he could deal with it, but he liked her. Just thinking about her made him smile. How did he ignore that feeling?

Lennox Hill Hospital occupied a prominent place on the Upper East Side. Lara stood outside one of the labor rooms at the nurses' station. One by one the newborns were wheeled out of the room and down to the nursery. In blue scrubs, his mask hanging at his throat, Derek wandered down to the nursery.

Donning a mask, Lara followed him. "RDS?" she asked when Derek was listening to one of the baby's lungs with his stethoscope. The respiratory distress syndrome was sometimes a common complication for a baby born preterm.

"No, he sounds good. He'll need an oxygen hood for a while."

She released a big sigh.

"Who's the pediatrician on record, Lara?"

She made herself meet his gaze. Trapped by it, she felt her pulse quicken. "Dr. Bryman."

"He's good." He straightened, looked so tired but smiled at her. With a look, he skittered sensation through her. "When is he supposed to show up?"

"His service said he was on his way," she answered, striving for an all-business tone.

"How are the Halverson triplets doing?" He ambled toward one of the cribs containing a newborn who was wearing a pink cap.

"Wonderful." Lara knew what he was doing. He was stalling, checking on the others while he waited for Dennis Bryman to arrive. "I'll say good-night, then." They'd been too busy for either of them to mention the near kiss. But she knew she wouldn't.

At the elevator she looked back. His deep-set eyes locked on her again. Her heart beat harder. Was he remembering the kiss? She hoped so.

Derek figured fate had taken control, thrown him and Lara together last night. If they hadn't been stuck in the elevator, he wouldn't have kissed her.

"It's not too hot to go, is it, Daddy?" Joey asked, grabbing his attention.

It was miserable outside. New York was caught in an unbearable heat wave. High temperatures had hung around for days. Humidity burdened the air. "To go where?" he asked, trying not to think about Lara. He poured cereal, then milk into a bowl for his son.

Joey pushed several of the chocolate, doughnut-shaped cereal pieces around in the milk. "The zoo."

"That's up to Dorothy." A widow in her mid-sixties, she was ample-figured with salt-and-pepper-colored hair and a dimpled smile. Unsure if the heat might bother her, he suggested. "Why don't you wait until my day off, and I'll take you then, Joey?"

Derek slapped a minimum of butter on a slice of toast. Could he rush his son? He'd been running late since he'd awakened. He felt out of step this morning. That was Lara's fault. Inch by inch, tension had crept through his body during that kiss. He'd wanted to devour her. Why her? he wondered now.

The differences between them might be why he felt the attraction. They had different backgrounds, different outlooks. No, there was more. He liked her smile, the quickness of it. He liked her walk, the sound of her laughter and her conversations that went on nonstop sometimes.

"Daddy, Dorothy said we could go see that new movie. It's really good. Everyone says so."

Derek focused on them. "Everyone" probably meant Joey's best friend, Austin and Rylyn, the femme fatale of kindergarten. "Okay. We'll go to the zoo on my day off." Derek drained the last of the coffee in his cup and left Joey and Dorothy talking about the movie.

In passing he shut the kitchen drawer and grinned. He'd never look at a turkey baster the same way again.

After a scheduled caesarian at the hospital, Derek strode toward the doctors' lounge. He changed into a black polo shirt and charcoal-colored slacks, then grabbed a cup of coffee. He was draining the last of it when he heard footsteps behind him.

"I've been looking for you." Rose's gray eyes smiled at him, but he felt nothing for his ex-wife except affection for a good friend. Trim, at forty she still had All-American cheerleader looks.

"New hairstyle? It looks good."

She settled on a chair across from him and threaded fingers through the light-brown hair cut to just below chin length. "Thank you. I've been wanting to talk to you for days, but when I stopped by last night to pick up Joey for his sleepover with me, you weren't home."

"I was stuck in an elevator."

Amusement danced in her eyes. "Be serious."

"I am."

"Alone?"

Why would she ask that? "What does that matter?"

"Were you alone?"

"No, my nurse and I left late and got stuck. And don't make anything of it. I could have been stuck in there with the janitor."

"Well, she's certainly a lot more interesting."

Unbelievably so. "Joey tells me you're dating," he said to distract her from more questions about him and Lara waiting for rescue in the elevator.

"No one you know." A serious, almost worried look settled on her face. "Derek, I need to tell you something."

Instinctively his stomach tightened. She wasn't smiling.

"I'm leaving."

He'd never liked surprises. He liked this one even less than most, he decided as she explained herself.

"To spend time at the Paris Institute will be a marvelous opportunity for me."

He knew it must be or she wouldn't go. "What about Joey?" he asked while he dealt with a mixture of emotions: pride, annoyance and disbelief.

"I'm not worried about him. You're a wonderful father."

"But you won't be here when he needs you."

She turned a sad look on him.

Don't look at me like that. She didn't have to say anything. He knew what she was thinking. Because he'd had a rotten childhood, he believed Joey might have one if she wasn't around for a while.

He'd already broken a promise he'd made to himself when his son was born. He'd vowed Joey wouldn't go through what he had as a child. So much for promises. He and Rose had divorced, shattered their son's family.

"Derek, Joey is well adjusted. And this will be good for him in one way. He'll only be living in one residence for a while." Rose gave him a weak smile. "I'll tell him when it's almost time for me to leave."

Joey deserved better than what they were giving him.

Derek couldn't get that thought out of his head. He left the hospital and crossed the street. He had a three-o'clock appointment at Manhattan Multiples with a woman who'd recently received the news she was expecting three or maybe four babies.

Inside the center, he rode the elevator to the third floor. Rose would explain to Joey what was happening. A simplistic solution. Nothing was that simple. If Joey was upset, he'd come to Derek for answers. And children were resilient. At an early age hadn't he learned how to handle disappointment?

"Dr. Cross, you have a call on line two," the appointment clerk said as he strode by.

With a nod, he hurried into his office and grabbed the telephone from his desk. "Derek, it's your father."

Annoyance rose within him in a flash. What could his father possibly want?

"I'll be in town for a few days. I thought we could meet."

"Where are you now?"

"I'm in Acapulco."

He'd thought his father was in Europe with wife number four. Alone? Derek wanted to ask, but why bother? He'd never really known his father's last wife.

"I'll call you when I get in," his father added before hanging up.

Brief, to the point. All of their conversations were the same. Why the stopover in New York? It had been years since they'd seen each other.

Even before his mother had died, he'd never known the love and affection from his parents that Lara felt from hers. Maybe that was why envy had fluttered inside him when she'd talked about her family. Dumb thinking, he decided. His family was Joey now. His son was all he needed.

The moment Lara entered the center, Josie and Carrie cornered her. "We have a plan."

"For you," Carrie said, pointing a finger at her.

Lara stopped at the front desk to scan the next hour's appointments. Oh, great. "What plan?"

"For your problem. You know about—" Nearby footsteps silenced her.

Derek nodded his head in their direction, then settled at a counter nearby and scribbled notations on a patient's chart. Few could decipher his chicken scratch. Lara numbered among those few.

Carrie whispered, "I've talked to several of the nurses who work at the center and the hospital and friends you have here. We've decided your problem is real."

Lara slanted a look at Derek. She'd swear the edge of his lips had twitched in a grin at that announcement.

"So we'll help."

"Help?" Lara decided she'd better concentrate on Carrie. "Help how?" If standing on a street corner and wearing one of those signs that would advertise for a husband was part of their plan, she was refusing.

She was thankful Derek had chosen that moment to leave. He stood at the end of the hallway, talking to his ex-wife. Possibly he still had feelings for her.

Perhaps that's why he'd avoided involvement with other women.

"We're all—"

"How many of you are there?" Lara asked Carrie.

"Eight. We're going to hunt among friends—male friends—and our relatives to help you find your Mr. Right."

"Wait—" What was she going to say? Don't do this. Why? This was exactly what she needed if she was serious about having a baby. She'd depleted her own resources for an interesting man, someone she'd want to spend the rest of her life with. Because despite the urgency she felt about having children, she wouldn't act impulsively. Mancinis married for keeps.

On the stairwell, they joined Allison Baker. "Eloise announced she's going to throw a small fundraiser this month for Manhattan Multiples."

"I don't understand how the mayor can even consider cutting funds to us," Carrie said as they entered the staff lounge.

Lara agreed. The center provided prenatal care, counseling service, fertility specialists, day care, yoga classes and meditation for mothers-to-be. While Lara liked the mayor, she wondered if Bill Harper's motives for making Eloise's life miserable weren't personal. She'd heard gossip that they had had a past. Lara didn't know if that was true.

"I'd love to go to the fund-raiser," Carrie said.

Josie shook her head. "I doubt we'd provide the kind of donations Eloise is looking for."

"Too bad," Carrie murmured. "It would be an excuse to buy a new black dress."

Josie shrugged. "I don't own one."

"You look wonderful in what you do wear," Lara said because Josie leaned toward denim everything.

Josie beamed back.

Inside the staff lounge, a crowd had gathered around a small television screen in a corner.

The mayor was being interviewed by a local news station reporter. A tall, lanky man with salt-and-pepper hair, Bill Harper had the bluest eyes Lara had ever seen. He smiled slowly. "If Eloise Vale really believes I'm doing this to her center for personal reasons, we need to talk. If she has the courage to face me," he said smiling.

"Eloise won't be pleased," Allison said, suddenly, joining them. "That was as good as a dare." Allison's chin-length, auburn hair swung with the shake of her head. "I feel so badly for her." People all over the city are poking fun at the feud between Eloise and the mayor."

Lara stared at the television. The mayor and Eloise put on their happy faces for the public, but Lara couldn't help wondering if there wasn't more behind the feud.

After leaving them, Lara returned to the second floor and slipped a patient folder into the slot on the door outside an examining room, then strolled back to another room.

The mother-to-be wasn't showing yet. Still slender,

she offered a weak smile, though she looked pasty. "I'm told the nausea will pass soon."

Lara touched her arm. "It will."

While the woman wandered down a corridor toward an exit, Lara went into the examining room. She hadn't expected to see Derek still there. She prayed for no awkward moments between them.

"She needs iron supplements," he said without looking up from the sheet of paper before him. He yawned, then cast a grin her way.

"You're tired?" Her voice wasn't quite steady even to her own ears.

"Late delivery last night. I'm used to no sleep."

To avoid meeting his eyes or seeing that grin, she stared at his hands, strong yet gentle. She'd seen them touch with care, caress a baby's head, bring new life into this world. She'd felt their strength and tenderness. "You'd have more time if you didn't spend so much time at Manhattan Multiples," she said to focus on something else.

"So would you."

Leaning back in the chair, he looked so comfortable with the moment between them. She wasn't. An undercurrent of awareness rippled through her whenever she looked into those eyes. "The center is so vital to the community." She wondered if he felt an inkling of anything when he looked at her. "I hate the idea that they might cut funds to it." She believed a woman in a high-risk pregnancy with twins or higher-order multiples needed the special attention the multifaceted center offered.

"Too bad you and I can't convince the powers that be." He made another notation on the chart before him. "What's new with the husband hunt?"

"You won't believe what happened." Get busy, quit staring at him, she told herself and turned away to pull at the used paper sheet on the examining table. "I can hardly believe what they're doing. Carrie and Josie talked to friends of mine at the hospital." Lara tore off the sheet, balled it and tossed it into a receptacle. "They've decided to help me find Mr. Right, fix me up with dates."

His silence made her look up. "Is that okay with you?"

Don't think about sneaky jolts of desire. "I think it's really nice that they're doing this."

He frowned as if he didn't think it sounded too wonderful.

She laughed to make light of the plan. "When Carrie said she knows someone who's free tonight, I said yes before I chickened out. Her number-one candidate is a lawyer with the district attorney's office. How can I turn them down? Maybe I'll find Mr. Right with a little help from my friends."

He didn't return her smile. "Is that a traditional way your family would approve of?"

"Oh, sure. In Italy that's all there used to be. Pre-arranged marriages."

"When you first started here, I thought you were seeing someone."

She was surprised that he knew that about her. "I was." She'd wasted three years on James. "He was a stockbroker. We didn't do well.'' Like James, Derek came from a different world.

Pushing back from his desk, Derek stood and grabbed the patient's chart. "I'm sorry."

"I'm not," she said easily and truthfully. "He was all wrong for me."

"It's good you realized that before it was too late."

As his breath whispered across her face, her throat went dry. "I didn't." She paused, took a breath to soothe her nerves. "He did."

Unexpectedly he leaned forward, touched a strand of her hair near her cheek. The touch, though casual, was like a caress. "He was a fool."

Sensation rippled through her. He had only to lower his head. Heart pounding, she told herself not to make too much of what might have been nothing more than a comforting gesture from him. Of course, it was more, she mused. Light, tender, it had felt like a caress. "We have one more appointment?" She made herself step back. "After, I'd like to leave right away for a date." She started to turn away, but stopped herself. "You never mentioned the kiss."

"Impulse," he said simply. "Sorry."

Was this his way of telling her the kiss had been a mistake?

"Have fun on the date."

She frowned. "Thank you," she said breezily to give the impression she was looking forward to the evening ahead. But she already wished it was over. The man she wanted to be with was standing right in front of her.

Chapter Four

The date was terrible.

To relieve stress, Lara awoke early the next morning and stopped at a dance studio near her home. Though she'd given up her acting career, she'd never abandoned her practice routines because dancing was a love, a joy in her life. She stretched, warmed up, then rushed through a routine she'd seen in the movie *Flashdance* until she was breathless. After a cooling down period, she headed home to shower and dress for work at the center.

If only last night's date, Zack Benner, had quickened her pulse. What she wanted most was to find someone special to build a life with, to raise children with, to love. Zack was not that man.

So who was she looking for? She didn't expect the

man to be perfect. Handsome would be nice, but just attractive would do. She'd known a male model who couldn't pass a store window without stopping to preen.

She would like someone with a nice sense of humor, who laughed at himself, who was amused by small things in everyday life. But she'd never been keen about a practical joker.

She wouldn't turn away from a charmer, someone who sent flowers, took her to romantic candlelit restaurants, but she'd favor more someone who was steady and responsible and paid the bills.

Derek fit her idea of perfect. He was drop-dead gorgeous, had a wonderful sense of humor, possessed all of the social graces and had money, to boot. He even thrilled her with a look.

Nearly at the entrance doors of Manhattan Multiples, Lara slowed her pace in response to the ring of her cell phone. Before saying hello, she'd guessed who was calling. Only her family tracked her down before eight-thirty in the morning.

Her sister Angela rushed a quick, airy hello, one that put Lara on the defensive instinctively. Angie's previous matchmaking efforts had been disastrous. "I called to learn if you bought a new dress for Danny's wedding," she said.

Lara didn't dare admit that she'd forgotten about her cousin's wedding. "Not yet." More important to her was who she'd take with her. "How is the baby?" she asked as she left the elevator.

"That tooth came through this morning."

"Oh, how wonderful. How many does that make?" Lara asked and paused next to the nurses' station to finish the conversation.

"Six. He has six. He bit Tom yesterday. What does your doctor say about biting?"

"My doctor isn't a children's doctor." She resumed walking toward the staff lounge. "He's an ob/gyn."

"That's right. Why do I keep forgetting that?"

Because it's your way of mentioning him.

"I couldn't believe how handsome he is."

Lara remembered. Her sister had sat gaping when Derek had walked by their table during one of their sisterly lunches. "I know." Lara tucked her shoulder bag into a locker. "You told me."

"And he's still unattached?"

"Still unattached."

"Lara, I'd be happy to cook lasagna or my chicken primavera or anything you'd want. You could invite him here for dinner and—"

"Angie, thanks but no." She left the staff lounge. "He's not interested."

"In you? Is he blind? Why wouldn't he be interested in you?"

"In anyone here," Lara said, hoping that would end the conversation.

"Oh. Why didn't you say so right away?"

Lara knew she was getting the wrong idea, but it was easier to say nothing. "I have to go now. I'll call you later this week," she said at Carrie's approach.

"Why didn't you tell us?" Carrie asked in a loud whispery voice.

"Tell you what?"

"That you were stuck in the elevator with *him*."

Mentally Lara groaned.

"Everyone is talking about it."

"When the lights went out," Lara said with a casualness she didn't feel, "it was a little creepy for a while."

Carrie smiled. "The lights went out?"

This was getting worse. "Carrie—"

"I'm teasing," she said with a laugh. "How was the date? Did you like Zack? Isn't he great looking?"

And dumb, Lara mused. "Is he really an attorney?"

Carrie squinched her nose. "He hasn't passed the bar exam yet. That's really difficult, you know. But he does work as a document clerk at the district attorney's office. What did you think of him?"

"Interesting," she said noncommittally. To avoid more talk about him, she waved goodbye on her way to the door, then hurried forward to usher a patient into an examining room.

At Lara's announcement that Derek wasn't there and another obstetrician would see her, the woman frowned, but a tease colored her voice. "Dr. Cross isn't supposed to have days off."

I miss him, too. Lara kept the thought to herself, but that didn't stop her from thinking about him during the next few hours. No matter how hard she tried, she couldn't forget those moments with him. And then what about yesterday? Why had he touched her? Perhaps she was making too much of a gesture that meant nothing to him.

She returned to her station off the hall of examining rooms. Taking a seat behind the counter, she spotted a lab test Derek was waiting for and pushed buttons to print the results.

"Hello, Lara."

Looking up, she smiled at Derek's ex-wife. "Hello, Dr. Clayson."

In her early forties, she appeared younger because of a faint sprinkle of freckles across her nose. "I haven't seen you in a week. Are you working more hours at the hospital?"

"No, I've been here." Though staff had scheduled hours, the doctors often were late or called back to the hospital because of emergencies.

"Congratulations, Rose," another doctor called out as he passed by.

Something great must have happened to her. "I guess I should be congratulating you." Lara sent her an apologetic look. "But I don't know why."

"It hasn't been officially announced yet. I've been offered a position in Paris." She mentioned a research facility known for ground-breaking accomplishments.

"That's wonderful."

"I'm quite excited." As her name was called over the center's paging system, she smiled. "Talk to you again."

What had Derek thought about the news? Lara wondered. Rose Clayson's decision to leave the country had to affect him and Joey in a big way. Standing, she snatched up the printout and pivoted away from the computer.

"I hope that's what I'm looking for," Derek said suddenly behind her.

Lara leaned back against the counter to give him her full attention. If only he'd kiss her again. Then she'd know he'd really wanted to. "Isn't this your day off?"

"We detoured from our trip to the zoo."

She noticed now he was dressed in jeans and a white polo shirt. Her gaze shifted to Joey, standing beside him.

"Is that Kelly Johnson's lab report?"

Dedicated. She would like someone who cared above and beyond what was expected of him. "Yes." She set the printout in front of him, then reached into a desk drawer. "Hi, Joey." Quickly she rounded the counter toward him. "This is for you."

As she handed him the red licorice twists, his eyes brightened. "Those are my favorite, Lara."

"Mine, too."

"Good news here."

"Yes." She looked up, had expected him to be reading the lab results. Instead, his eyes were on her. "No diabetes." Lara vowed to be relaxed, act normal today. *Act.* There was the key word. She'd act normal, unaffected by him even if he stood close to her.

Joey tugged her hand. "Do you want to go to the zoo with us?"

"Oh, I wish I could but I can't leave yet." She really did wish she could.

"You could eat with us later." Joey swung a questioning look up at Derek. "Couldn't she?"

"Joey, Lara probably has other plans." Derek sent her an apologetic look. "A date."

"I have one later on this evening." It was now or never. "But I'd love to go out after I finish work." She couldn't believe she was doing this. She looked at Joey, then bent down to his level. He was why she'd been brave enough to agree. "Will you come back for me?"

"We will, won't we, Daddy?"

Derek's eyes locked with hers. "Are you sure?"

Don't act too anxious. "Yes, I'd really like to—"

"We'll be back in a few hours."

"Okay." She actually had a date with him. Them, she reminded herself. Derek wouldn't have asked her. This was all about Joey. Well, that was okay, too. She liked him, would enjoy being with him for a few hours. But she needed to keep her imagination in check, not pin too many hopes on the time they were together.

"Joey, why did you do that? I told you she wasn't my girlfriend." Already Derek viewed this as a mistake. Why had he agreed? But then why hadn't he called her for lab results instead of stopping at the center? Why was he forcing more time with her?

Joey shot him a wide-eyed, confused look. "You like her, don't you?"

Was a preference for red licorice enough of a common thread to bind two people? "I like her." He'd wanted to see her, wanted to know about the date. Last night he'd gone to sleep wondering about her and the guy.

"Why couldn't she go with us, then?"

If only everything was so simple. Derek touched his son's slender shoulder. His smallness always made him feel an intense need to protect. He wanted nothing to hurt him. "She can be our friend," he said to remind himself she wouldn't be more.

Trust filled the blue eyes staring up at him. He expected so much, Derek mused. Every day he prayed he wouldn't let his child down. "What do you want to see first? Monkeys?" He caught his son's hand in his. "Elephants?"

"Lions."

Derek chuckled. They always had to see the lions first.

"Where are we going to eat?"

Derek reached down, sought a sensitive spot on his rib cage. "Your favorite place."

Joey squealed with Derek's tickle. "Pizza."

At his son's laughter, he lifted him into the air and onto his shoulders. "Pizza."

Spending more time with Lara probably wasn't the smartest thing to do. But then neither was a day at the zoo in the middle of summer.

Hot. Derek promised himself he wouldn't do the zoo bit again at this time of year. Keeping an eye on his watch, he made certain he and Joey returned to the center in time for the end of Lara's shift.

"You look warm," she said when she approached them in the reception area.

He felt sweat on the back of his neck, but wasn't entirely sure it was only because of the warm temperature. She looked great in snug jeans. "I kept wondering whose dumb idea that was," he murmured low, not wanting Joey to know he hadn't had a good time.

Lara gave him a sympathetic look. "Poor Daddy."

Amused, he played along. "I'd appreciate a little more compassion in your voice."

"Wait. I can do this better. I'm used to more than one take," she said lightly, referring to her acting career.

He reached around her to open the door. A faint breeze greeted them with oppressive heat and humidity, but he caught a hint of her perfume again. The scent reminded him of spring flowers after a rain. "How was last night's date?"

"He was a friend of a friend."

Sun shone on her hair, turned blond strands silvery, tempted him to touch. "Blind dates aren't usually easy."

"Every person you date is a stranger at first."

Lazily he dragged his eyes from her tight backside and long legs in the snug, faded jeans. Joey stayed only a few steps ahead of them. "Did he do dinner and dancing?" He wanted her to confirm that she'd had a miserable time.

"Dinner."

Had she invited him into her place? As quickly as the thought formed, Derek discarded it. She wouldn't do that after a first date. So where had they gone? Muscles in his back and neck tensed. His stomach burned. Jealousy. He recognized the emotion now, knew he had no right to the feeling. There was nothing between them.

"Lara!" a female voice yelled out.

The distraction helped, stopped him from getting caught looking at her backside.

A couple dodged traffic to cross the street to her.

"Jodie! Neil! It's been so long," Lara squealed and rushed forward to the curb to hug a tall man with longish dark hair and a Lincoln-style beard and his companion, a petite, curly haired redhead.

Derek kept Joey with him to give her privacy. As their chatter rose an octave with excitement, Derek couldn't help smiling. Lara was so passionate about people. Too much so, he mentally grumbled while he watched her hug the man again.

Looking delighted, Lara walked back to him and Joey. "Friends. From the theater. We were in a Broadway musical together ages ago. Maybe a decade. He's doing Lincoln off-Broadway." Squinting against the sunlight, she stared up at him. "And she's doing a stint on a soap opera. It was so great seeing them again."

She flashed another smile, made his throat go dry. How did she manage to bother him so much without doing anything? "Do you miss that? I remember you told Mindy Richards that you don't, but do you?"

"When did you hear me—oh, during one of her checkups. You remember that?"

She had no idea how much he knew about her. He remembered everything he'd ever learned about her since she'd begun working at the center. He knew she liked hot-fudge sundaes and Italian food and old musicals. "What happened with the acting?" he asked after they'd entered the family restaurant. A perfect choice, he thought. Romantic notions had no chance with the sound of kids screaming and bells dinging on pinball games.

"Daddy." Joey tugged at his arm while he eyed the kids jumping around with excitement in the ball pit.

Derek spent the next few minutes buying tokens and ordering drinks and pizza while Lara found a table near the racing game Joey was playing. He shouldn't be here with her, shouldn't get involved with her, he knew. Yet he approached the table with one need—to feel her in his arms again.

"He's having fun," she said.

Derek nodded. One taste. Just another taste. He frowned with annoyance at himself—at her. He should never have agreed to this. Talk. Don't think. Don't feel. "Tell me more about when you were acting."

She leaned an elbow on the table, rested her cheek on her fist. Looked sexy. But then, to him, she'd looked sexy in her uniform when she stood beneath fluorescent lighting at the center.

"In the beginning, I auditioned everywhere and landed bit parts. Then I had a chance at a Broadway musical. I was in the chorus." Her eyes danced with pleasure. "I loved it. But I never got a lead part, except in an off-Broadway play."

He'd heard she'd had a chance at the big-time. "You were in a few movies, too."

She stared at his son, not him. "A few."

"I saw them," Derek admitted.

In a way he found charming, she tipped her head at him. "Did you really? What did you think? Be honest."

"I thought you were good." He'd thought she was beautiful, talented, exciting. "So what happened?"

She shrugged. "It was less than what I wanted to do with my life. When my dad became terribly ill and was in the hospital, one nurse was awful to him."

"That can happen."

"I know. Not all nurses are caring. But he also had some dedicated, wonderful ones, and I felt what they were doing was more valuable. Nursing was a natural for me."

Curious, he wanted to know more. "In what way?"

"I always loved caring for people. When one of my sisters or brothers got hurt, I'd run for the Band-Aids. While I was going to school, I joined a Big Sisters program for a while. Even while acting, I'd volunteered at nursing homes in between my acting jobs. I finally realized I was born to be a nurse. I was a late bloomer,'' she said on a laugh. "I was in my late twenties before I went back to school and became an R.N. All of my friends thought I was crazy.'' She went silent for a second. "I'm talking too much, aren't I?''

He couldn't help smiling. "Who said?'' She returned a faint smile, a thank-you. It amazed him that she didn't realize he liked listening to her talk.

"Did you always want to be a doctor?''

"Going into medicine had been expected of me. My grandfather was a doctor. So was his father.''

"Derek, that's nice.''

What had he said to stir that response from her? "What is?''

"That you continued the family tradition of practicing medicine.''

"I liked it, so that helped.'' He'd realized there was nothing else he'd rather do, or he'd have turned his back on family tradition. "Where were you working before Manhattan Multiples and Lennox Hill?''

"I worked for a while in pediatrics. When I heard about Manhattan Multiples, I switched to obstetrics. I love the idea of multiple births, that two people can become a family of four or five or six on one special day in their lives. I hope one day I'll be that lucky.'' She looked up as an adolescent boy materialized at their table with the pizza. "Do you want me to get Joey?''

"I will.'' He pushed to his feet. How long had it been since he'd spent so much time talking with a woman, been so interested in all she had to say? How long had it been since he'd felt so content just listening to a woman?

"Daddy, look how good I did," Joey insisted when Derek came up behind him.

"Wow!" He lifted his son off the seat. "How did you get to be such a good driver?"

"I watch you. Can I go back after I eat?"

Derek urged him toward the table. "In a little while." Lara had set a slice of pizza for Joey on a plate to cool. "But sit now and eat."

"I did real good, Lara," the boy announced not too modestly.

"Well," Derek corrected, sitting again.

Joey shot a funny look at him. "What, Daddy?"

"Well."

"Well, what?"

Across the table, Lara giggled in her napkin.

Derek stifled a grin. "I'm glad I did so well."

"Me, too. Would you play Pac-man with me after we eat?"

"Can I do it?" Lara asked.

Mouth full, Joey nodded.

"Great," she said with a glance at her watch.

"Hot date?" Annoyance filled him that she was mentally gearing up for a night with another man.

She smiled wide while cradling a slice of pizza between her thumb and index finger. "It's just a date."

Without warning, the dark mood deepened within him. "How many of these do you have planned?"

"I could have one every night for the next month."

"Every night!"

Lara released a short laugh. "My friends took my problem to heart."

Oh, hell. Though uninvited, the green-eyed monster perched on his shoulder again. Deliberately he led her, hoping she'd answer with a complaint about the dates. "Aren't you getting bored?"

"No, they've been interesting."

The weight on his shoulder grew heavier.

"It's interesting, though."

He didn't like thinking about her with other men. He kept expecting her to breeze into the center one day excited because some man had thrilled her the night before. "What's interesting?"

"Different people have such different ideas about what perfect is. My sister chooses dreamboats. And it's not that good-looking men don't please me." Head bent, she dabbed a napkin at her fingertips. "Some do, but not the ones who tell me it takes them an hour to shower and shave."

"Daddy does it in ten minutes. He times us," Joey piped in.

"I don't time us."

"Uh-huh," Joey said, nodding his head for emphasis.

Derek thought an explanation might dig him out of the hole his son was burying him in. "He has a time limit because he likes to play in the shower in the morning."

"I've heard you're a stickler about time."

Damn, he sounded like a fuddy-duddy even to himself.

"You should come see the games, Lara," Joey said, taking control of conversation. "They have a fishing game. I like to fish. Do you?"

"I'm a city girl," Lara said. "I've never gone fishing."

"Daddy could take you, too. You wouldn't even have to touch the worm."

"I wouldn't? Why wouldn't I?"

Joey bent his head close to hers and whispered conspiratorially. "I have him do it for me. He would do it for you, too."

As if he wasn't there, she whispered back, "Are you sure?" She sent Joey a warm smile.

Derek had seen other women flash smiles and pretend interest in his son to impress him. Not her. He could have not been there. The attention his son was receiving was genuine, he realized.

"Daddy, you would put the worm on for both of us, wouldn't you?" Across the table, Joey nodded his head to prod for the right answer.

"Absolutely."

"Told you," Joey said.

Derek's smile widened. They looked cute with their heads bent close as they carried on, acting as if he wasn't there. They looked right together.

Now there was a dangerous thought.

Pinball was her game, Lara knew with no modesty. Even as a child, she'd beaten her brothers and sisters at the game.

"You won, Lara," Joey said excitedly minutes later.

Lara stepped back from the pinball machine. "Barely. Harvard Medical doesn't teach pinball," she teased Derek. His face was near. With a tilt of her head, she could have pressed her lips to his. "How did you get so good?"

"It's a requirement to ease stress in a doctor's spare time."

The noise, Joey, the family atmosphere had kept her nervousness around him at bay for a while. "I never heard of that before."

"You're good, champ."

"Thank you." Lara told herself not to make a big deal about his touch, but his palm was against the small of her back, his mouth near her ear as he tried to be heard over the noise. Repeatedly she fantasized about this kind of moment, feeling his touch, even casually, but had never imagined a time so special with him and his son.

"Joey, you can play another game. We're going back to the table."

"You and Dr. Clayson have done a great job with him," Lara said as they ambled between tables to their own. "You try so hard to make everything nice for him, even though you're divorced." She didn't care if she was out of line. People like him and Rose, who put their son above their differences, deserved a pat on the back.

"Thanks," he said, sitting across from her. "When Rose got pregnant, we tried to make the marriage work, but even though Joey means everything to both of us, he couldn't bind our marriage together. We tried for his sake. But failed."

She knew what a perfectionist he was. He'd hate failing at anything. "How did you meet?"

"During medical school we fell for each other. Rose was a fellow resident. We had a lot in common." He looked down for a moment. "We were both ambitious, wanting to be the best doctor in our fields."

Had ambition hurt their marriage, or something else? As much as she wanted to know, she couldn't ask him. "I heard about Dr. Clayson's news," she said. Unsure what Derek's feelings were about Joey's mother leaving the country, Lara had deliberately not said good news.

"It's something she's always wanted."

Lara heard a hint of disapproval in his voice.

"She'll work at a prestigious medical research clinic in Paris. They're doing genetic research to prevent birth defects."

Lara tipped her head. "Important work. That's good news. Isn't it?"

"Of course it is." The way his back straightened indicated he thought differently. He raised his head, met her stare. "I guess I'm not doing a convincing job at hiding my concern."

Such candor from him stilled her. He was usually

more private. This kind of closeness had to mean something, didn't it?

"Yes, it's good news for Rose."

For Rose. Unspoken words were heard. He wasn't in favor of her plan.

"Joey will miss her."

And he wanted to protect him from any kind of hurt.

Derek glanced at his son. "I hope he understands. It means that she'll be gone for a while."

Lara didn't want the door shut again. She hesitated, then realized that she couldn't play it safe and not ask more. "For a long time?"

"A year. Rose thinks this might actually be good for Joey. He'll be able to live with only one of us for a while."

"He seems to be one of those amazingly adaptable children who goes with whatever is happening."

"Some kids don't have choices. We already put him through divorce."

"Children bounce back very well, Derek." Instinct led her. She reached across the table, touched his hand to comfort. "Joey doesn't seem unhappy or withdrawn." As he looked down, she took her hand away. She knew enough about him to be aware he didn't lean on others. In fact, she couldn't recall any moment when he expected something from another person, or indicated he was depending on someone to do something or be somewhere.

"It wasn't fair to him. I'd never do that again to another child."

Lara thought he was being too hard on himself, but clearly he blamed himself for the divorce. She didn't know if it was his fault, but she'd learned that no one was totally to blame. She'd seen her brothers scrap during their growing-up years, and always they were both at fault in a fight. She'd watched one of her sisters struggle to keep her marriage going, and knew firsthand that Christina and her husband had both lacked a willingness to compromise until they went to counseling.

"Daddy, can I get more tokens?" Joey asked, suddenly beside them.

Derek shot a quick grin at him and dug into his pocket. "Here are a few more. But that's all. You're almost done."

She was, too, Lara mused, scowling at her watch. She was *not* looking forward to another blind date.

"You have to leave?"

Lara looked up. Had she imagined the disappointment she heard in his voice? "I should." Though reluctant to go, she gathered the straps of her shoulder bag.

"What's planned? A movie? Or what?"

"Maybe a movie."

"You don't know?" he asked, standing and looking as if having no plans ranked as a criminal offense.

"I suppose we'll be spontaneous."

In what she viewed as an impulsive action, he slid a hand around hers as if to keep her near but held it for only a second. "Don't you ever make definite plans?"

Lara was slow to answer. "Not too often." In retrospect she wondered if that attitude was the reason she was still single and worrying about motherhood. Other women planned their futures better. "I learned it at my mother's knee," she said, trying to make light of what she thought he might view as a fault. She knew he organized everything, even the paper clips in his desk according to size. "When you come from a big family, you need to adapt all the time. Someone is always changing plans."

"As a kid, everything was always planned for me."

"Do you do that with Joey?"

A self-deprecating grin curved his lips. "No. Joey's his own man."

That was because he was a good father. He didn't try to restrict his son's actions too much. That said a lot for Derek. "Thanks for inviting me, Joey," she said when he dashed to them.

"You're welcome. Want to come with us again?"

Lara looked Derek's way. Say something, she urged silently. He said nothing. Even a wink would have been sufficient encouragement. "We'll see, Joey," Lara answered.

"My daddy says that when he means no."

Derek winced.

Lara stifled a grin at his reaction. "I don't, Joey. I mean maybe," she answered but wanted to say yes. For the past few days, she'd been taken to a movie, a concert and romantic dinners. She'd had more fun at a pizza parlor with this man and their five-year-old chaperon.

Chapter Five

"You sound blue," Gena said in response to Lara's less-than-cheery greeting over the telephone.

Wasn't that just like Gena? She was going through her own torment, but still she worried about her. They'd been friends since high school. It wasn't often either of them could hide a problem in their life from the other. "The weather is dreary." Outside her kitchen window, rain plopped at a steady beat.

"Don't even try to kid a kidder. This mood is because of the doctor, isn't it?"

Gena was the only person she'd revealed her crush to.

"He doesn't want what I want. I know I'm fooling myself about him. Stupid elevator."

"What?" Gena asked, laughing.

"If the elevator hadn't jammed, then we wouldn't have spent time alone in the elevator, and I'd never have let myself—"

"Fantasize?"

"Boy, did I."

"Did he kiss you?"

"Yes. I'm such a sucker for single fathers."

"All women are. They're admirable. Rarely self-centered."

"Usually generous and thoughtful."

"Yep. That, too."

"And he's a doctor. A dedicated one, right?"

"Very."

"Lara, why don't you do what you always do? Go get him."

Lara laughed softly and shifted the receiver to her other ear. "I don't always do that."

"You always go after what you want. Why not this time?"

"He's my boss."

"Are you worried that you'll lose your job?"

"I could, you know."

"Are you exaggerating?" Gena teased. "You always did that, too."

"You know me too well."

"My pleasure." A smile filled Gena's voice. How courageous she was, Lara thought. "Lara, it's Sunday. You know where he lives, don't you? Go see him."

"I don't think so."

"Don't be so shy."

"Shy?" she said on a giggle. Was she acting that much out of character? No one had ever called her shy. Gena was right. By nature she went after what she wanted.

After making one stop, she hailed a taxi and went to Derek's home. She rode the elevator to his floor, but several times while crossing the gray-carpeted hallway, she stopped and took calming breaths. Even at the door, she debated with herself about how wise this was. Doing a quick count to ten before she changed her mind, she pushed the doorbell.

Standing before her, he looked stunned.

"I came with breakfast," she announced in a rush before she lost her nerve.

"Lara?" Joey yelled from somewhere inside. "You came," he said, suddenly standing beside his father. "Just like you said you would when we were in the park."

"Yes." She raised the bakery bag close to Derek's nose. "Smell. Croissants, doughnuts and Danish."

"Just like you said?" Derek muttered, repeating Joey's words. "I'm feeling like odd man out. What are you two talking about?"

"In the park Lara said she knew a place near us to buy good doughnuts. Chocolate-chocolate doughnuts," Joey added, eyeing the bag.

At least one of them was happy to see her, Lara mused.

"You know one of my son's weaknesses."

Though he said the words pleasantly enough, Lara

suddenly wasn't so sure she'd done the right thing. "I hope that was all right."

Over Lara's shoulder, Derek peered into the white pastry bag. "What kind of Danish?"

They ate breakfast on the terrace where Joey entertained them with a story about a classmate who tried to lap up his milk like a dog.

"They're five years old," Derek reminded her.

"I know some adults whose antics aren't much better," Lara assured him.

Cradling a cup of coffee, he leaned back in his chair. "Ah, you dated a dud last night."

Was it her imagination or did he sound pleased? "Yes, he was." She scanned the sweeping expanse of windows in the living room that offered a stunning view of Manhattan skyscrapers. "This is nice."

"Thanks."

The decor was ultrasophisticated, black lacquer and plush furniture. The walls and sofas in a neutral shade complemented the large nineteenth-century Japanese screen in the same neutral beige along with black and varying shades of brown that hung on a wall behind one sofa. Black touches at the base of the lamps, black inlaid wood on end tables, a baby grand piano.

After taking the tour of their apartment, Lara decided she liked that Joey's room was a little messy and was done in a sports theme, mostly baseball. She'd noticed photos of him and Derek and Rose, and of a smiling elderly couple with the man holding a fishing pole, and one of a distinguished-looking man with silver hair who resembled Derek too much not to be his father.

When seated again, Derek motioned toward the array of pastries on a platter. "Thanks for bringing breakfast."

She nibbled at one on her plate. "I love the bear claws."

"Apparently my son does, too," he said with an askance glance at Joey. "Tell me about the date. Why was it so bad?"

"He slurped spaghetti into his mouth."

A laugh threaded his voice. "Terrible."

Slanting a sidelong look his way, she saw his grin. "This is amusing you, isn't it?"

He gave into a smile. "Yes. I tried to warn you. Blind dates are bad news."

"I'm beginning to agree with you."

"What else was wrong with the last one?"

He wasn't you, she could have said. Did he really care? Or was he simply looking for conversation to be polite? "We had nothing in common. He plays golf. I dance for exercise." She paused. "You're smiling again."

"What else was wrong with him?"

"He liked the sound of his own voice. And he likes mayonnaise with corn beef on rye. Silly thing to remember, isn't it? But doesn't that sound disgusting?"

"Disgusting."

She feigned a scowl. "You are having fun at my expense." She didn't mind. The light-hearted moments with him only convinced her more that he possessed most of the fine qualities she'd choose in *the* man for her.

Across from him, Joey wolfed down the last of the danish and his orange juice. "Lara, do you want to read a comic book with us? Dad's a real good reader. He talks in lots of voices."

"Joey, she—"

Lara stifled a grin. Daddy had many talents. "I'd love to." In her whole life, she'd never been this pushy. But desperation made her willing to try anything. "Daffy Duck is my favorite," she said and followed Joey.

They sat on the sofa, leaving a space between them for Derek.

"Okay." He laughed good-naturedly. "But you have to read Daisy Duck's part," he said, pointing at Lara. "I'll do Donald. Joey, you do Pluto. Ready?" he asked, plopping on the cushion.

"Ready," they said in unison.

Lara laughed at his Donald Duck voice. She would never look at Dr. Derek Cross in the same way again. Seeing him with his son proved what she'd known all along; he was special.

She sat back, listening to father and son take turns with Joey reading the easy words. This was what it would be like to be a family. This was what she yearned for most. She could be happy with them, she knew.

"We're going to the video store. Want to stay, Lara? Daddy always makes popcorn."

"Good popcorn?"

His face rounded with his broad grin. "The best. We're getting the new dinosaur movie."

Lara had read the review for the animated feature about a dinosaur with polka dots. The movie stressed that being different was okay. "I'd like to, Joey, but I have to visit my family. They're expecting me." Lara crouched down before him. "But I had a wonderful time."

"Us, too. Huh, Daddy?" His eyes darted to Derek for a confirmation. "She reads good."

"Yes, she does. Thanks again for breakfast," he said, walking her toward the door.

"You're welcome, I think." Her voice trailed off at the sight of his frown. What thought had brought that on? "You look annoyed."

"You're not making it easy, you know."

Tension tightened muscles in her back. "What do you mean?"

Featherlight, he touched her hair. "To stay away from you."

She wanted to smile. "Oh. Is that so bad?"

"Yes. I'm not the answer for you, Lara." Lightly he brushed strands of hair back from her cheek. "I'm not."

She managed a smile, nodded. "I'd better leave." Drawing a hard breath, she hurried out, not looking back. She could have stayed with them forever.

But she knew now that she wouldn't stop the blind dates. One of those men could be Mr. Right. As wonderful as Derek was, despite the fun time with him and Joey, Derek wasn't that man. He'd made it clear that he would never be.

At seven the next morning, in anticipation of the heat outside, Lara pulled her hair up and off her neck. All wasn't right with her world. Besides Derek's words to her yesterday before work, she had a doctor's appointment. She'd been forced to make it a few days ago.

Even when she'd sat in the waiting room, feeling her stomach knotted with tension, she'd drummed up reassurances, striving to keep her spirits up. Everything would be all right. The doctor would tell her she was worrying needlessly.

But he didn't. "Lara, your symptoms—the abdominal pains, the heavy periods, indicate we might be looking at endometriosis."

She battled an urge to cry. "I...I was really hoping you wouldn't say that."

"It's important to check this out now. You don't want it to worsen."

No, she didn't. She knew that it could hurt her chances to have a baby. "I have a friend who was told she might need a hysterectomy because of it," she said, still concerned for Gena.

"Well, let's not get ahead of ourselves. But we need to run more tests first and see if this is your problem."

Lara left the doctor's office, more worried than she'd revealed to him. Dealing with depression, she begged off lunch with co-workers, and went for a walk through Central Park. What-ifs plagued her. What if that was her problem? What if she needed a hysterectomy? What if her chance to have a child was gone?

No, she couldn't think that way. She believed a glass of liquid was half-full, not half-empty. She expected good things to happen. She couldn't believe her greatest wish in the world might be out of her reach.

By the time she entered Manhattan Multiples, she'd convinced herself that a pregnancy wasn't impossible. Until someone said there was no hope, she wouldn't give up.

"The Yankees won another one last night."

Lara pivoted around toward Derek. He stood with a shoulder braced against the doorjamb of his office. "I know." She'd assumed they would be back to a doctor-nurse relationship.

"Did you watch the game after you left us?" he asked, sliding a patient's chart into a slot at the nurses' station.

"I missed it last night because of a date. An unexpected one. My family's fix-up this time." No man should look so good, she decided. Under his white lab coat, he wore a midnight-blue shirt with a gray-and-blue tie and dark slacks. "After dinner they surprised me. 'I've invited a college buddy's brother-in-law,' my brother Mario said. 'Good guy. But he's more the bookworm type.' This from a man who thought anyone who couldn't catch a football was lame. But I caught the highlights of the Yankees' game on this morning's newscast.''

Derek looked past her as the door to the waiting room opened. ''Yesterday evening's date was…?''

She pulled a face. ''It was okay,'' she said, rather than admit it had been awful. Because of the wonderful time she'd spent with him and Joey, she wondered if she was being fair to other men. What choice did she have? He'd told her that he wasn't interested, hadn't he?

''Was the date with a guy who has glasses?''

''Glasses? Yes.'' Craig had one topic of conversation—bugs. A tall, thin man, an entomologist, he'd talked about them while driving and during dinner and at the elevator inside her apartment building. Even her doorman, Charley Simms, seemed aware. He rolled his eyes at her when they passed by. At that moment Craig had been discussing the mating cycle of the praying mantis.

''He's here, you know.''

''Who—Craig?''

With his nod, Lara groaned. ''Oh, no. What can I do?'' She needed to discourage Craig, but she didn't want to hurt his feelings. Staring at Derek, Lara struggled for a way out of the dilemma. ''We're friends, aren't we?'' That was the way he wanted everything between them, she reminded herself. Before she lost her nerve about an impulsive idea, she asked, ''Would you help me?''

''You know I would.''

She hoped he continued to show such agreeableness after she explained her plan. "Last night's date wasn't going well. I could tell Craig and I wouldn't—"

"Have a repeat performance."

"Yes, I knew I wouldn't see him again, and well—I kind of fibbed. I didn't want to hurt his feelings, so I told him I had an old boyfriend at work, and was having a hard time forgetting him, that I might go back to him. Look out there, will you?" she asked, touching the door.

He looked amused, too amused, but she had no choice. "Okay, what am I looking for?" he asked, opening the door an inch to do as she requested.

"Is anyone else out there?" Lara asked. It was imperative no one see them.

"No. There's no one else there."

"This is serious," she said in a pseudo-reprimanding voice.

"I know."

Meaningfully she arched a brow. "Then why are you smiling?"

"I have no idea." His smile widened. "Except you make me smile."

"Because I'm silly."

"Silly is all right, Lara."

Remembering his many voices while reading the book, she knew he could be silly. "But not right now."

He gave her his most serious look. "Okay. I get it. This is serious business." The smile dancing in his eyes belied his solemn tone. "What do you want me to do?"

"Pretend you're him for a few minutes."

"'Him' is the...?"

"Boyfriend. Pretend you're the boyfriend for a few minutes. I know what you said yesterday. I understand. This has nothing to do with us. It's about—him," she said and gestured with her thumb toward the door.

"Okay." He really sounded willing. "How do you suggest I do that? Put my arm around you?" He stepped closer. "Kiss you?"

Oh, he was serious, wasn't he? "Probably a quick kiss to send him a message to go on his way. It doesn't have to be long," she suggested. "A peck on the cheek will do." She was kidding, of course. In her heart she still wished he'd want more. "Five seconds."

"That'll do the job?"

"Oh, I'm sure it will," she said, aware there was danger in even one second. "No feeling is necessary."

He laughed. "No feeling?" he said in what she thought was a skeptical tone.

Oh, this was an impossible idea, she knew. In a slow, deliberate move, she inched the door open, peeked at Mr. Wrong. He looked so eager, so...pitiful. Of course, she couldn't kiss another man in front of him. "Never mind." She shut the door, drew a deep breath. "I can't do that to him. That seems cruel. I have to go talk to him,'' she said and flung open the door.

Derek watched her rush out of the room in the manner of someone who didn't want to take time and reconsider her actions. When she'd stopped a polite distance from the man, she smiled. She had a lot of different smiles. While this one was as genuine as the one she gave Joey, the sparkle wasn't in her eyes. But the guy didn't know that. He was smiling now, nodding.

Nice. She was nice, as beautiful inside as she was to look at. He shut the door and returned to his office to make notes on a new patient's chart. He'd have liked that kiss. Even a pretend kiss. A short peck, a kiss without feeling? He had to laugh. Never would he have stopped after a few seconds.

Nonproductive thinking, Cross. If he let feelings overshadow common sense, he'd do something idiotic. But he regretted his words yesterday, didn't want to push her away. He'd like to spend time with her, lots of time, intimate time. That was insane, he knew. Joey's existence demanded that he always consider the consequences of his actions now.

He hoped Rose still believed that, too. He'd always viewed himself as a patient man, but he also believed in charging forward and completing difficult tasks. Putting off an inevitable unpleasantness bordered on cowardliness in his mind. So when did Rose plan to tell their son about her plans?

''I'm back.''

Startled, he nearly jumped at the sound of Lara's voice behind him. He'd expected her to be gone longer.

"That went better than I'd anticipated."

Because she looked so relieved, he had to ask. "What did you tell him?"

"I explained that I might get back with someone I dated before. I didn't want to lie."

He moved out from behind his desk to sit on the front edge of it. "*Might* being the operative word?"

"Exactly."

"So no kiss is needed."

Her head snapped up. She looked speechless. A feat. She was prone toward talkativeness rather than silence. He placed a finger beneath her chin to close her mouth. It didn't matter what common sense told him. He wanted to feel her softness against him.

Lara released the breath she hadn't realized she'd been holding. "Do you want to kiss me again? I thought you said…"

"I was wrong. Say okay."

"Okay," she said a touch breathily as he put a hand at her waist and drew her close to stand between his legs. She didn't understand why he kept pushing her away if he wanted more. Maybe she was dreaming. No. This was real. She kept repeating those words until they sank in.

Touching helped. She placed a hand on his chest first, then slipped her arm around to his back. His lips caressed hers lightly, then once more as if testing.

Sensation skittered up her spine. Her knees went

soft. Breathing took effort. Skimming her hands up his back, she pressed her lips harder against his. She would never forget this moment. The silence around them. The coolness of the room.

She'd never forget his kisses. His taste was a part of her body and her mind now. She'd kissed others. Kisses and hugs came easily to her. She believed in affection. But this wasn't simple affection. His kiss blocked every thought but one. *I want you.* The words filled her mind, overwhelmed her.

Willing. Inviting. She moved her lips over his while she slipped fingers into the hair at the nape of his neck. For years she'd dreamed of being with him like this. She sought the taste of his tongue, the warm recesses of his mouth. An ache gnawed at her. A senselessness, a wanting overwhelmed her.

Desire coursed through her. It didn't matter what he said to her. She felt his need in his kiss, felt an unbearable hunger within her, couldn't think about anything except the heat spiraling through her. Heart pounding, she clung, felt a slow-moving ache intensifying.

His taste still lingering on her lips, it took a moment to realize he was pulling back. She didn't want it to end, to think about anything but when his body had been hard and warm against hers. "You said you weren't the answer," she murmured.

He lifted his hands from her. "I'm not," he said in a voice that sounded huskier.

How could he say such words after kissing her like that?

"Everyone knows you're looking for a husband, Lara. I'm not it. I meant what I said before. People in my family don't do well at relationships." He spoke softly as if he hated saying the words aloud. "I've already proven that with Rose. I cared deeply for her, but we married for the benefit of Rose's and my career. No other reason."

Lara never expected him to say that. They hadn't been in love. How could people marry and not be in love?

"Everyone knows what you want." The no-nonsense tone was back in his voice. "But I'm having a devil of a time leaving you alone."

Instinctively Lara tensed, anticipating that she wouldn't like what he was about to say. "What I want?"

"I'm not interested in marriage again. I'm not a candidate for your child's daddy."

A second passed before his words penetrated the haze she'd been under. "My...my child's daddy!" She saw red. Had he really said that? "That is— Talk about conceit." With effort, she fought to keep her temper in check. "Did I ask you?"

When he looked away, hurt sliced through her. How could he kiss her like that, then turn away as if she didn't exist? "You kissed me," she reminded him.

"And I want to again. But we needed to get this straight between us."

"Don't be concerned." Too piqued to say more, she started for the door, but stopped and whirled back.

"You don't need to worry about me," she informed him in her haughtiest voice. "As far as I'm concerned, we're just colleagues."

That was the most ludicrous thing she'd said to him. Derek stared after her. She was gone, the door slamming hard behind her. Well, the quickly thought-of plan to put her off before he weakened and did something stupid had worked. But dammit, he'd seen hurt in her eyes. Mentally he kicked himself. If he hadn't kissed her, what he'd said to her wouldn't have mattered so much, and she wouldn't be mad at him now.

He shouldn't have kissed her like that. But he'd wanted her, had longed to see passion in her eyes once more.

Now it wouldn't be easy working together. She'd be polite to him when they were around patients, but otherwise, he'd get the cold shoulder. That would be lousy. He liked the relationship he'd had with her before this.

He pushed away from his desk, snatched up a patient's chart, but didn't move except to set the chart down again as his mind countered previous thoughts. She wouldn't act differently. She was a professional. She wouldn't let personal feelings interfere with what happened at work.

Still he should have resisted temptation. This was all his fault. Every day, every moment with her ended with him yearning for more.

He considered himself a logical man. He analyzed,

reasoned out problems. Lara Mancini was a problem for him. She annoyed him, bothered him. Say it like it is, he berated himself. She made him ache.

So what if he leveled with her? A short-term relationship, no promises. And he wouldn't get in her way of finding what she wanted.

Damn, he sounded selfish. Why would she even agree to it? She wanted more, a lot more.

Miffed, wanting to punch something, Lara gave in to temptation and bought half a dozen doughnuts. She ate two of the jelly-filled ones on the way home.

With sticky fingers she handed the bag with the four other doughnuts to Charley, the doorman, a barrel-chested man with cropped gray hair and a gruff voice. He was retired military with a wife of forty-one years. "Got a problem, Lara?" Long ago she'd requested he not call her Ms. Mancini. She'd debated Yankee pitcher choices with him too often to expect formality.

"My sweet tooth kicked in," she said about the doughnuts. "That's all."

"Because you have a problem. A man?"

A man who deserved a dose of castor oil. Or something nasty. "A man. Enjoy the doughnuts, Charley." She marched into her apartment, wished she still took kickboxing lessons, but her dancing, an occasional night at the ball park and volunteer work at the center took up most of her time.

Some way, though, she needed to unleash angry

energy. With no other outlet, she grabbed a bucket and a scrub brush and slapped it at the kitchen floor.

That didn't help. The floor shone, and she was sweaty. But she still felt irritated. She showered, then dressed in jeans and a red tank top. After pinning her hair up in a black clasp, she headed outside. A threat of rain darkened the sky with heavy, pewter-colored clouds. The dismal weather definitely matched her mood.

"Going to get wet," Charley said when she passed him.

"That's okay." She couldn't sit, couldn't relax. She had to do something. What nerve Derek had. He'd acted as if she was chasing him.

"Lara!"

Only feet from her building, she swung around and was greeted by four smiling faces. Friends. She needed them more than ever. Besides Jodie and Neil, two other friends she hadn't seen in a few months, Casey and Jeremy, rushed forward for hugs.

"Look at this face," Jodie said, framing the angular-shaped face of the good-looking, lean male standing beside her. "Guess where he's going?"

The joy in Jodie's face for Jeremy roused Lara's smile. "Tell me."

"Hollywood. He'll be Freddie, the freeloader neighbor, on a new sitcom."

Thrilled for their friend, Lara hugged him hard.

"And you're coming with us," Jodie said, grabbing her hand.

"To go where?"

Casey, a slim brunette who'd been on tour with *Riverdance* gestured with her thumb in Jeremy's direction. "To celebrate his good fortune."

"We need you to help us celebrate," Jodie declared.

And she needed them, Lara realized.

They took a taxi and settled into a large corner booth in an Irish pub where Jeremy's cousin was a server.

"I only want a glass of wine," Lara said. "Neil, you're best at toasts."

"Are you toasting my good fortune or drowning your sorrow?" Jeremy questioned.

"My sorrow?" Head bent, she pursed her lips to make a face. "Don't be silly."

"Someone is bothering you. Tell us," Neil urged, hunching forward over the round table they were sitting at to put his face in her vision.

"It's that one you were with, isn't it?" Jodie questioned.

"He's arrogant and annoying and—everything," she said between sips of the wine.

"Ah," Casey said.

"What's 'ah'?" Lara asked.

Neil smiled. "*Everything* is the important word."

"Tell us more about your man trouble," Jodie urged.

"I'm not having men trouble."

"But you are having *man* trouble, aren't you?"

Lara frowned at her empty wineglass. "I seem to need another."

"Oh, this is serious," Jodie said, but she kept on smiling. Elbows on the table, she rested her chin on her hands. "She needs another wine," she told the server.

Lara moaned. "I'm probably going to regret that in the morning."

"It didn't look as if he wasn't aware of you the other day."

"What about the other day?" Jeremy questioned.

"They were together," Neil said to help the others play catch-up on what they viewed as a romance.

"I was 'together' with his five-year-old son, too," Lara reminded him and took a hearty swallow of her second glass of wine.

Jodie laughed. "You're getting plastered."

"I'm not."

"You're slurring."

"I'm done," she said, pushing the wineglass away. "Remember the words to the chorus of 'Gonna Wash That Man Right Out of My Hair.'"

Casey only needed a reminder of when they were all together in the off-Broadway version of South Pacific. She hadn't sung three notes when Jodie joined in. Neil and Jeremy added their voices to the song and forced the rest of the patrons to be their captive audience.

Too many drinks, plenty of songs and, after more than one round of applause, they finished with "New York, New York."

"We'll see you home," Neil insisted as they stood under a streetlight.

"No, I'm fine." Light-headed, Lara pointed. "I'll hail a taxi."

Being with them had helped ease the hurt she'd felt from Derek's words. But despite the hours that had passed, she thought about his words and felt irritated all over again. He'd insulted her, she thought with full-fledged indignation. "How dare he?" She leaned forward. "Driver. I changed my mind. I need you to take me somewhere else," she said, then rattled off Derek's address.

Chapter Six

A kiss. Who'd have expected any woman's kisses
to haunt him. Dressed in a sleeveless gray T-shirt and
black bike shorts, Derek exercised on the rowing machine while watching a video of the scenery along the
Rhine. His vision blurred with the image of another.
Lara, eyes nearly closed, lips parted. With his blood
pounding and her slim body against his, he'd been so
close to letting go. Too close.

Under his breath, he swore, and rowed harder. The
rumble of thunder, the patter of rain against the window pulled him from thoughts of her. He glanced at
the clock. "Five more minutes of exercise," he said
to himself but managed only one more.

The doorbell buzzed once. A short, quick buzz. He
rowed slower three more times. When the doorbell

buzzed again, longer, he stopped, wondering who was leaning on it. Muttering to himself, he grabbed a white hand towel from a nearby chair and ran it over his face while he crossed to the door.

He wasn't expecting anyone. Joey was with Rose for the night. Derek had a buddy, a photo journalist, who tended to drop in without calling first, but he'd been working out of the country for several weeks. A neighbor, an elderly man, sometimes stopped by simply because he was lonely and wanted to hear another voice, but he had a lady friend over tonight.

Be more flexible, Cross. People claimed he needed to relax more. He did when he was with his son. And Lara. He hadn't spent such a lazy Sunday with anyone except Joey in a long time. Derek tossed the towel aside and opened the door.

Without a greeting, Lara stormed past him and into the room, stopped by the wall of windows and swung around. "I've come to tell you off."

It took effort not to smile. "You have?"

In a rush of energy, she circled his living room. "Yes."

He couldn't think about anything except how enticing she looked in the tight jeans, skimpy red top, and flimsy-looking sandals. Her face was flushed, her hair tousled from the wind. Without looking back, he shut the door. He couldn't take his eyes off her, wondered if she'd look like this after a night of love.

She sent him a look. He assumed she meant to deliver a glare. Instead she looked slightly cross-

JENNIFER MIKELS   101

eyed—and cute. "You have a lot of nerve, you know."

Rain had dampened the top of her hair, dotted her face, spotted the shoulders of her blouse. "Do I?"

"Yes, you do. You don't know everything."

"I guess not." He was so tempted to place his hands on her wet face. "So are you going to tell me?"

"Someone needs to put you in your place." She took a step. She'd have walked a line perfectly, if it was crooked.

Derek reached out to steady her, but she held her own without him, so he dropped his arm to his side.

"How could you believe I had some plan to trick you toward marriage?"

"How many drinks did you have?"

"Two," she said, holding up four fingers. She stared at her fingers and frowned, and with her other hand pushed down two of her fingers.

More, he assumed. "You're tipsy."

"I'm annoyed." She got in his face. "With you."

"I gathered that."

"I came here to tell you—" She poked a finger at his chest. "To tell you off. You're so smug. So superior."

"Am I?" This wasn't like her. He knew she'd felt hurt, but the woman he'd worked with wouldn't let some man's words unbalance her. What else had happened today?

"Will you stop answering with questions? Yes, you are."

How could he find out what really was wrong? "Lara, is your family okay?" he asked, unable to think of anything else that might have upset her so much.

"You're still asking questions."

"Are they?" he insisted.

"They're fine." A strange tenseness strained her features. In the blink of an eye, her mood gave way to another. A look of misery slipped over her face. "I'm not, Derek. I'm not okay."

Concern rippled through him. "What do you mean?" A heaviness settled in the pit of his stomach. "Why aren't you okay?"

"It wasn't good news at the doctor's."

A health problem? How could someone who looked so fit have one? "You went there for what reason?"

She didn't deserve whatever problem was coming her way. A sweet, beautiful woman with a generous, compassionate heart deserved a charmed life.

In a less-than-coherent way, she gave him a replay of what the doctor had said. " 'It's important to check this out now. You don't want it to worsen,' he said. And I said that I didn't. But I have this friend and she needs a hysterectomy, and I could have the same problem, and now we need to run more tests." She finally took a breath, tears filling her eyes. "All I could think about was that I might never be able to have a child. I want one. I really do, Derek. Some women don't care, but I do."

Unexpectedly she buried her face against his shoulder. His arms went around her. Every time he met a woman with this problem, he wished for more knowledge, for a way to give them what they wished for most. A miracle for some. Miracles were out of his reach. He couldn't do more than draw on all of his knowledge and skill. When miracles happened, they had nothing to do with him. "He's correct, Lara. More tests need to be done first. Don't upset yourself. You might have no reason to be so concerned."

"I know, I know." Sniffing, she drew back. "I know. Don't worry."

He nearly smiled. She sounded so young. "You'll be a great mother, Lara. No matter how you become one."

With another sniff, she brushed at the dampness on his shoulder. One emotion had led to another. If she hadn't drunk too much, he didn't think she would have revealed her problem.

"We'll be friends again. Okay?" she said thoughtfully. "Friends are nice." She gave him a mellow-looking smile and offered her hand.

Humoring her, Derek took it to accept her handshake. Could they be just friends now? He knew her taste. He knew what he'd be missing.

A frown wrinkled her brow. "You're damp," she said about his shirt. "Why are you damp?" She skimmed fingers down his upper arm to his biceps.

With her caressing touch, a slow burn inched through his gut. "I was rowing."

Swiveling away, she listed slightly while she scanned the room in the manner of someone trying to orient herself and unsure of her surroundings. "Rowing? Outside, you mean? In the park?"

"No. Here. On a rowing machine."

She shook her head as if it was too muddled to decipher what he was saying. "Oh." Though she bobbed her head then, he doubted she understood. "I should leave," she said softly.

"It would be better if you stayed." He placed hands on her shoulders even as temptation rushed him to yank her against him again, to take another kiss. She had no idea how much he'd like to spend the night with her.

"Stay?" Her brows bunched. "You want me to stay?"

He didn't like feeling so unsettled whenever she was near, but right now wasn't the time to change anything between them. "Come on."

"Where am I going?" Her legs gave way on the last word.

As she sagged against him, Derek bent over, then gathered her into his arms. "I know a bed that's calling your name."

Coiling her arms around his neck, she giggled. "That's ridiculous." A small frown deepened the faint line between her fair brows as if she was struggling to think clearly. "Beds don't talk."

With his foot, Derek shoved open the door to a guest bedroom and carried her to the bed. She felt light in his arms. He was aware not only of soft curves but also of how toned she was. He was aware of too much. Gently he lowered her to the mattress. "You can sleep here tonight."

Her arms still tight around his neck, she held him nearly in a choke hold. "Derek, I need to tell you something."

"What?"

"You're a great kisser." Her eyes closed for a second. "I feel fuzzy." Sleepy-looking eyes met his again. "Do I look fuzzy?"

Smiling, he reached up for her wrists. When he loosened her grip on him, she dropped her head back to the pillow and closed her eyes. "You look beautiful," he whispered.

Wearing filmy white, her blond hair flowing back from her face, the woman was delicate, ethereal, her skin velvety soft. As her pale arms stretched out, her palms up toward him, he moved closer. Aroused now, he needed only to take a few more steps, then she'd be in his arms again. He'd recapture the pleasure.

One more step. Just one. He never took it. Sound annoyed, distracted. He looked away from her. For a second. No more. But when he looked back, she was gone. The dream was over.

The ringing shrilled louder, demanded his attention. On a curse, Derek buried his face beneath his pillow even as he reached for the telephone receiver. He fumbled for a second, then peered in the direction of the phone. Predawn grayness greeted him. "Cross," he mumbled, noting the time on the digital clock.

"I'm sorry to bother you, Dr. Cross, but one of your patients was brought into emergency."

"Who?" Fully awake now, Derek swung his legs out of the bed.

"Sarah Ellis. She was in a car accident."

Standing, cradling the portable phone between his jaw and shoulder, he yanked up his slacks. What injuries?" he asked while he snagged a shirt from a chair.

"She has a cracked rib."

As he listened to the emergency room doctor recap Sara Ellis's vitals, he paused at the door of the guest bedroom. Lara was gone. "The fetal monitors are in place?"

"Yes, they are."

Buttoning his shirt, he headed toward the door. "Be right there," he said, and left the phone on the foyer table.

Mortified. Lara groaned while she stood under the shower in her bathroom.

She remembered her tirade. Something about "arrogant." She winced. Had she really said that to him? What else? What else had she said? Done?

She remembered black shorts. They'd clung to his backside and muscular thighs. She remembered muscular arms and how sexy he'd looked in the shorts and the sleeveless gray T-shirt.

She remembered feeling such despair.

She remembered resting her cheek against his shoulder. With her hand on his chest, she'd felt the steady beat of his heart through the thin gray T-shirt. She hadn't realized how badly she'd needed closeness with someone until he'd wrapped her in his arms. The tension of the day had flowed out of her with his comforting warmth.

She remembered his touch, his compassionate embrace. Mostly she remembered being in his arms. He'd carried her to a bed. Wasn't that every woman's fantasy? A great fantasy. She'd felt breathless from his nearness as he'd bent over her. His face had been close, the light caress and warmth of his breath near her lips. If only she hadn't passed out.

She'd awakened in his home with a headache—and fully dressed except for her sandals. Nothing had happened except she'd made a fool of herself. To avoid awkward moments, she'd left for home before dawn.

Humiliated, her head pounding, she downed a few aspirins. To counter dehydration, she drank a quart of water. She remembered she'd had several drinks. Who knew how many?

With a coffee cup in hand, she was about to flop on a sofa and vegetate in front of the TV when the phone rang. Gena's call delivered more bad news. Lara snatched up her shoulder bag and dashed for the door.

The moment she left the elevator at the hospital's maternity floor, she spotted Derek standing at the nurses' station. Warily she approached him, unsure how he'd react to her this morning. All the way over, she'd debated with herself, and had finally decided to act as if this was like any other day.

In his blue scrubs, he finished making a notation on a chart, then looked up, frowned. At her? No, she saw concern in his eyes. "You're not here for your hospital shift, are you?"

"No. I heard about Sara Ellis from my friend Gena."

"She's still in ICU, but she and her three fetuses are all stable and doing fine."

Lara released a sigh of relief and moved to stand beside one of the computers behind the long, white counter.

"She would probably like to see you."

"I plan to visit her. Gena and Sara and I went to high school together. I was so surprised when she showed up at Manhattan Multiples," she said more brightly than she felt. She'd be all right once the aspirins dulled the pounding in her head. "Well, I'll go—" She backed away, aware she was rambling. "I'll go see her before I leave for the center."

"Lara, how are you feeling?"

She gave up the pretense and the phony smile. "I've been better." She narrowed her eyes now because it made her head hurt less. "Thank you for letting me stay the night."

"Why did you leave?"

"I...I felt like a fool. I acted dopey."

He shifted his stance to face her squarely. "I said more than I should have."

She might not remember much after her celebrating

with Jodie and the rest, but she had no trouble re-
calling what he'd said to her earlier yesterday about
trying to nab a father for her child. "I hope you don't
really think that I—"

"Lara, we need to back up a few steps."

"Yes," she said agreeably. How did she stop this
longing for him? "About what happened at your
place—"

"Nothing happened."

"Except I bawled on your shoulder and said too
much and—" she sent him an apologetic look "—I
don't know why I told you about my health problems.
I have no excuse. I'd been drinking with friends. Actually, more than one drink is too much for me, but
friends asked me out, and I needed—"

"To relax," he finished for her as if sensing how
stressed out she'd really been.

She thought that was an understatement. "Become
comatose is a more apt description. Anyway, I wanted
you to know that I appreciated what you did for me."

"Lara, it's all right." They were skirting what had
really happened. "You're worried."

"I am." She couldn't deny the obvious. "I've been
trying hard not to let it get me down." She paused,
tried to settle her nerves before she asked the big
question. "Everything is a little fuzzy. Did I say anything that would make me cringe?"

"Nothing." His answer came too quickly.

And why was humor sparkling in his eyes? He definitely wasn't telling her everything, Lara decided.

* * *

After leaving him, she spent an hour with Sara, assured her she'd be home soon, and wouldn't deliver her babies too early. When Sara's husband came in, Lara left. In the hallway, she saw Sara's parents. After hugs, they played quick catch-up about their lives.

Happy after seeing old friends, she was feeling a lot better as she left the hospital to head for Manhattan Multiples than she'd felt when she'd arrived. And her head no longer had tiny men pounding away at it.

Crossing a street, she withdrew her cell phone from her purse. She'd barely switched on the phone when it rang.

In response to her hello, her sister Angela announced, "Lara, Rosa's pregnant." Her cousin Danny's fiancée had four sisters—Sophie, Maria, Nancy and Rosa.

Lara hit the entrance doors to Manhattan Multiples. "No, she isn't the one who's pregnant," Lara said, certain her sister had mixed them up.

"Yes, she is."

"Rosa, too? Oh, my gosh, Angie, that's incredible."

"I know. I know. That's five out of eight bridesmaids."

Lara glanced up. Derek stood at the elevator, waiting for her. "I have to go now, Angie. I'll call back later."

In a studying manner, he watched her. "You're frowning."

"That was my sister." She joined him in the elevator. "Angela. The one you met at the restaurant that day months ago who sat with her mouth hanging open. Well, she called about my cousin Danny's wedding."

"A big wedding?"

"Eight bridesmaids." Despite what he'd said she was convinced she'd done something foolish at his home. "Linda—that's the bride-to-be—wanted ten, but Danny said eight was enough." She laughed.

"My sister called to tell me that another bridesmaid is pregnant. That means five of the eight bridesmaids are," she said, moving to the opposite wall. "Six are married. The other two are still in high school. One won't show. But four of them are out to here." She held a hand three inches from her stomach and laughed softly as an image flashed in her mind. "My aunt has been going crazy with the alterations on the dresses. Every time she turns around, one of them has gained three more pounds."

Derek smiled with her. "Sounds interesting."

"It does, doesn't it?" This was better. They weren't as tense. "One problem. I don't have a date for the wedding. And in my family, for a single woman to come to something like this without a date is unheard of. Most of them are already convinced that I'm destined for 'spinsterhood,' unless I marry Aunt Connie's friend's nephew, the sanitation man."

"The sani—"

Lara nodded. "The sanitation man. And if I'm alone, they'll be pinning an Old Maid card on my back. Or I'll hear, 'So, Lara, when are you getting married? Getting older, Lara. You shouldn't wait too long, Lara.' You get the idea, don't you?''

"Why don't you have a date with all those men being thrown your way?"

"Thrown my way?" Why was it that every time they discussed the blind dates he said something that pushed her buttons?

"Never mind," he said, raising a halting hand. "What about one of them?"

"My family will embarrass him. Oh, Lord, can you imagine? Want to hear how conversation will go if I do bring someone? 'Lara, who's your boyfriend?' Remember now," she said to Derek, "this is about a guy I've dated once. I can hear my aunts. 'Do you believe in a long engagement?' 'She's not a girl, you know.' Any man I've dated is still a stranger. He might take their words seriously."

A corner of his mouth lifted in a wry grin. "Sounds as if you need a friend to take you. You did say we'd be friends again, didn't you?"

Friends, she mused as she stepped out of the elevator first. Was he really offering to go with her?

"Lara!" Carrie's voice sang. "These are for you."

"Me?" She frowned as she neared the counter at the nurses' station and spotted the vase filled with yellow daisies, baby's breath and several daffodils. Yellow daisies.

"An admirer?" Derek asked.

Lara reached for the card. "They're from my sister's man of the hour. She told him that I was a sucker for yellow daisies."

"You are?" Carrie asked. "I didn't know that."

"Neither did I," Lara said lightly. "It's my sister who is a sucker for them."

On a giggle, Josie said, "She should date him."

"I think her husband and baby wouldn't approve." With the flowers cradled in her arm, she walked beside Derek toward his office. She wasn't forgetting what had sounded like willingness on his part to go with her to the wedding. "About Danny's—"

"When is the wedding?" Derek asked.

Lara released the breath she'd been holding. "You really want to go?"

Absently he fingered one of her hoop earrings. "Your aunts won't bother me."

"Okay." She couldn't block the tiny thread of hope that was weaving through her. "And I could introduce you as a friend," she said to see how he'd react to that term. He presented what she thought might be a pained look, but she wasn't certain. "That will work, then."

She watched his gaze lower and focus on her lips. She was dying to feel his arms around her again. "If you say so." A lightness, as if he was laughing at himself, had edged his tone.

What wasn't he saying? "It's what you want, isn't it?"

He arched a brow. "No, it's what you said you wanted."

What did he mean by that? "I did?"

He delivered one of those knee-buckling smiles to her. "Before you told me I'm a great kisser."

She had no chance to say more. Had she really insisted they be friends? Only friends after saying that?

At lunchtime Lara made her announcement to Josie and Carrie about no more blind dates.

"What was wrong with them?" Carrie asked, pausing in moving her French fry through the puddle of ketchup on her plate.

Lara waited to take a bite of her hamburger. "One examined his image in every shop window we passed."

Carrie giggled. "Allison picked him, didn't she?"

Lara gave her a backhanded wave. Placing blame for dreadful dates wasn't her goal. She was grateful to her friends for trying to help her, but it was time for them to stop.

"I've never met a man who did that."

"He told me he usually allowed an hour to get ready." She knew another man who could look gorgeous in ten minutes, according to his son.

"So what was wrong with the others?" Josie asked, abandoning her lunch, a grilled chicken breast and cottage cheese diet plate.

"You don't want me to give you details about the bug man."

Carrie made a distasteful face. "I've never liked bugs."

"He can enthrall you with information about the tiny ones clinging to your skin."

"Oh, stop!" Carrie begged.

"Not all of the dates were awful, were they?" Josie asked.

Lara was honest. "No, they really weren't. A few were nice and one was downright sweet."

"I hear a silent *but,*" Josie said.

Lara couldn't tell them that she felt guilty accepting dates when she wanted to be with another man. How could she tell them about her feelings for Derek? "I want to thank both of you. You're dear friends, but no more. Okay? I have one more tonight. Another friend of a friend of one of my brothers. Then I'm done."

"Okay," Josie said.

"I'll agree, too," Carrie said. "On one condition. If I find a really great guy that I don't want, of course, I get to send him your way."

Lara smiled and agreed, but she already knew a really great guy.

They finished lunch, and while walking back to the center, talked about skipping lunch one day and shopping, instead. As Carrie stopped beside Josie's desk in the reception area, Lara hurried toward the elevator, leaving them to discuss where they should go.

She breezed in and out of several rooms on the second floor and checked supplies. As she'd thought, more swabs and gowns were needed in one examining room. With time before the next patient, she left the room and pushed a door to climb the steps to the third floor. Besides offices, the supply room occupied a place at the end of one hall.

From a third-floor hallway, she heard a feminine

voice, "If you really cared about the citizens of this city, you wouldn't even consider such a budget cut." Eloise Vale stood and held her cell phone tightly against her ear. She was wearing a gray pin-stripe suit and a black silk blouse that emphasized the blond streaks in her chin-length ash-blond hair.

"You can't close this center," Eloise said into the receiver.

Lara stopped, uncertain if she should proceed or turn around. She never meant to intrude on a private conversation. The mental debate was unnecessary. Eloise suddenly clicked her cell phone closed and went into the supply room. Reaching the room herself, Lara slowed her pace. From the doorway, she saw Eloise. Head bent, she looked troubled, lost in thought. Lara cleared her throat, not wanting to alarm her.

With an annoyed frown, Eloise whirled around. "Oh, Lara." Her expression immediately gentled.

"Is something wrong?" Lara asked.

"Besides the Honorable William Harper's single-mindedness?" Frowning, she gave her head a shake. "Never mind, Lara. Forget I said that. He's unimportant."

The lady doth protest too much, Lara mused.

Eloise pivoted around, moved several bottles on a shelf. "I know some prenatal vitamins are missing from stock." She shot a look at Lara. "Why would anyone take them, unless she was pregnant? Do you know if someone on the staff is pregnant?"

Lara was honest. "I don't know." She wished she could say that person was her.

After placing supplies in room two, she wandered to the nurses' station, then stepped into the bathroom to change for her date. The last prearranged one.

"Lara." Carrie came out of a bathroom stall. "Did you talk to the patient Rebecca Newman a moment ago?" she asked.

"I didn't know she was here. She wasn't scheduled today."

"I saw her talking to the dietician on the second floor and getting information about the hospital for her insurance company. I thought she wasn't feeling well," Carrie said while washing her hands. "When is she due?"

"Soon. Another week maybe. Triplets."

"I suppose if something was wrong she would have made an appointment."

Lara nodded and unzipped the garment bag she'd carried in.

Carrie whistled at the jade-green-silk slip dress.

"Sexy dress. You're going to wow someone."

Lara looked up from putting on the black, high-heeled sandals with their crisscrossing straps and laughed. She'd like to wow one particular man.

Chapter Seven

Flowers. Men hanging around at the reception area. What next? Derek wondered. Despite what she'd said about no more dates, he expected one of her blind dates to show up at the center with a violinist or a mariachi band to serenade her.

And what about him and her? She'd seemed tickled pink about calling them friends. That damn word was definitely beginning to annoy him.

Muttering under his breath at his own contradictory thoughts, he opened the door of his office to talk to a new patient. A few moments later the woman who'd worked with a fertility specialist expressed her joy and astonishment. "My husband and I are trying to imagine having that many at one time," she said because of the news that she was carrying five babies.

"It takes time," Derek assured her. He talked about her making an appointment with the center's dietician. "You'll do fine because you're getting the right start."

"I can keep exercising."

"Walking is great exercise." He stood to see her out. "Make the appointment and pick up the vitamins." Derek opened the door for her.

"Goodbye, Dr. Cross," she called back, then headed down the hallway away from him.

"Have a nice weekend, Mrs. Anderson." Smiling, he turned and shut the door behind him. He stopped in midstride, wondered if he was gaping. Wearing a sexy little, green number with skinny straps that just skimmed the tops of her knees, Lara stood outside the staff lounge. She had great legs. Really great legs. He'd never noticed before. Well, he'd never seen that much of them before. "Hey." She was deliberately trying to torture him, wasn't she?

She strolled—sauntered on those stiletto heels toward him. "Do you need something?"

Loaded question. How could she walk in those heels? "No," he managed to say, and watched her until she disappeared into the elevator.

Lara leaned against a wall inside the elevator and placed a hand to her chest. Beneath her palm, her heart pounded. With his eyes on her, she'd felt suitably seduced, had struggled not to tug at the hem of her dress. He sure knew how to look at a woman.

She stepped from the elevator and smiled with her

new knowledge. She'd made him feel, she realized. Plenty. Dr. Derek Cross had done more than just look. He'd ogled her.

Still smiling, she crossed the center's reception area, saw Josie standing by her desk and waved good-bye. Steps away from the double glass doors, she heard the elevator doors open for someone else.

"Lara! Oh, my gosh," Josie yelled and pointed behind Lara.

Lara spun around. Standing outside the elevator, a hunched-over Rebecca Newman hugged her round belly. Distress twisted her face in a pained expression.

Even before Lara rushed to Rebecca, she saw the small puddle on the floor.

"My water broke, Lara." Panic edged the woman's voice.

"It's okay," Lara said soothingly to calm her, and slipped a hand under Rebecca's elbow to usher her away from the elevator. "You're with a lot of people who can help you." She steered her toward a chair outside a staff meeting room door.

"I know I am, but—" She paused, winced.

Lara glanced at the clock on the wall near the reception desk. "Who's picking you up? Your mother or husband?"

"Husband," she said while Lara helped her into a chair.

Kneeling on the floor beside her, Lara grabbed her hand. "Is that your first contraction?"

"No. No, it isn't."

"Josie," Lara called out.

"Dr. Elcot is gone," she said about the doctor handling Rebecca. "I already called Dr. Cross." She eyed the wet spot in elevator one. "And maintenance."

"Oh." Rebecca gasped at the pain, took another deep breath.

Lara began timing the contractions. "When did the contractions start?"

"I guess early this morning. I thought they were stomach cramps. Lara, my cell phone is in my purse. I need to call my husband."

"What else can I do, Lara?" Josie asked, hovering near while Lara handed the cell phone to Rebecca.

"Call an ambulance, Josie, and get me a damp cloth, please."

"At Lennox Hill," Rebecca told her husband. Her face was flushed, sweaty looking. She handed the cell phone back to Lara. "Another one's coming."

Lara dabbed at the perspiration on Rebecca's face.

"Lara, I don't think—" Rebecca pressed her lips together, gripped Lara's hand harder.

"Dr. Cross is coming off the elevator," Josie said, playing lookout at the door for the ambulance.

From steps away, Derek called, "Big day, Mrs. Newman." His voice was calm, upbeat, unconcerned. "Guess those guys of yours are anxious."

He hid his concern well, Lara mused. But a small line between his brows deepened. It was a telltale sign. Lara knew why without words being spoken. The closer Rebecca Newman got to her due date, the better.

"The ambulance is here," Josie announced from her watchful position by the windows.

Lara held Rebecca's hand while the paramedics transferred her to a gurney.

Rebecca winced again, death-gripped Lara's hand. "Dr. Cross, will you stay with me?"

Derek's hand closed over Rebecca's other one. "All the way to the hospital." Pivoting around, he smiled at Lara. "Thank you for staying. I can see you were supposed to be somewhere."

She expected him to move away, but he caught her wrist. "Lara."

Her pulse scrambled beneath his touch. A tiny tremor fluttered her insides. "What?"

"You'll take his breath away."

Take his breath away. Stunned, she managed a smile. Her heart banging in her chest, she turned to head for the exit. Outside, street sounds filled the air. All she heard were his last words.

Despite the date and another man's attention, Derek invaded her mind repeatedly. That's why she tried so hard with Kyle, a bodybuilder type with curly dark hair. Still, because of an early-morning shift at the hospital, she insisted on going home by eleven.

Mr. Macho was agreeable. "That's a good idea. I'll come in for a while and…?" He let the last word come out on a raised note, an indication he expected more.

Peripherally Lara saw Charley inching forward from his station at the door to come to the rescue.

She lifted a hand to motion for him to stop. She needed no rescuing. "I'm not inviting you up. I have to go to work early tomorrow," she said to ease the rejection.

"Hey, baby, you look too—" Cocky and slightly intoxicated, he grinned and spread his arms out as if taking in the whole picture. "You are a hottie."

As he lunged, she sidestepped him.

Standing on a step, Charley charged forward, caught him before he fell on his face. "I'll get you a taxi, fella."

"Nice move," a familiar male voice said behind Lara.

Her family would have been dumbfounded. She was speechless. She released an unsteady laugh as she watched Derek amble toward her. "This is a—"

"Surprise," he said with a self-deprecating grin. "I was running and decided to see if you were home yet." He released a short laugh. "That's a lie." His voice softened. "I'm here because I couldn't stay away."

Excitement and confusion filled her. He couldn't stay away? While he helped Charley ease Kyle into the taxi, she fretted. Now what? Should she push for more about what he'd admitted? Should she say nothing? "Did you mean what you said?" she asked when he joined her beneath the streetlight.

"That I was running?"

Despite the shadowed light, she saw the tease in his eyes. "No, I can see you were." She noted he was wearing a gray T-shirt, sweatpants and sneakers.

"I meant—never mind." She was not going to act foolish. "Joey's not home?"

"No. He's with Rose tonight." A smile tilted the corners of his mouth. "When he's not home at night, I run."

Because he misses his son, Lara guessed.

Unexpectedly he took her hand. "Want to walk with me?"

Something was different, was definitely happening between them. "Yes." She stopped trying to resist her feeling for him. This was more than a crush, a simple attraction.

He glanced down at her heels. "Can you walk in those?"

"Oh, sure." No way was she ruining the look with a pair of sneakers.

"Day after tomorrow, he and Rose are visiting her parents before she leaves the country." In an easy, casual move as if it was the most natural thing in the world to do, he brushed some strands of hair back from her face.

Warmth curled in her belly from his caress. Was he aware of how susceptible she was to his slightest touch? Was this, whatever "this" might be for him, happening because he'd stopped fighting the attraction? "It's hard when Joey's not around, isn't it?"

"Yes." He inclined his head questioningly. "You sound like someone who knows that feeling."

"After I lived with James for a while," she answered, "it was difficult to be alone. But one day he said it had been a mistake. I should have expected it, but I hadn't.'' She felt such disgust with her own naiveté. "What he didn't say was that I didn't fit in.''

Beneath a corner streetlight, she saw his frown. "Fit in?''

Lara didn't really want to relive that time. It hadn't been the happiest in her life. "Visits to his family were always stiff, conversation strained. I wasn't right for James Braden III.''

A hint of sarcasm edged his voice. "Braden?''

"You know James?''

"The Bradens are overly protective of their blue blood. You meet all kinds,'' he quipped. "Like your muscle man tonight.''

"He was different.'' As they turned a corner, Lara glanced away.

The owner of a neighborhood deli, Milton Rosen, a balding man in his late fifties with a Santa Claus shape, paused locking the door to wave at her. "Night, Lara.''

"Good night, Mr. Rosen,'' Lara called out. She turned her attention back at Derek. "Great food there.''

"I'll remember that. Tell me more about Braden.'' Clearly he wasn't being sidetracked.

"Obviously my background and his didn't mesh,'' Lara said. "You haven't met my family, but let me tell you my relatives are loud, definitely pushy, sometimes obnoxious and totally lovable. But he had told me he loved me, and I'd believed him.''

"I don't know about your relatives, but I can tell you that the Bradens don't approve of too much.''

"His mother informed me that this had more to do with me than them. I really wasn't suitable."

"She said that, in those words?"

"Candor was her best quality. She didn't mince words when she said—" She stopped, not wanting to repeat what else the woman had said, not wanting to remember hurtful words. A dream had been lost that night when she'd recognized how shallow, how self-absorbed James and his family were. He'd been totally unconcerned about how she'd felt.

Derek tipped his head to place his face in her vision. His eyes softened with a need to understand. "When she said what, Lara?"

She stretched for a smile. "It doesn't matter anymore. I'm glad you took your run this way."

"I told you I came this way deliberately."

He's not interested in marriage or being a daddy again, he'd said. He'd also told her that he wanted to kiss her again. Even as she knew he wouldn't offer everything she longed for, she wanted him to come upstairs with her. She wanted him to be her lover. She couldn't skip this chapter in her life if it meant spending time with him. "I'm glad you did."

Gently he skimmed knuckles across her cheek. "Lara, I could hurt you."

Maybe if she understood him better. "Why would you believe that?"

"You want things I'll never consider," he said even as he kissed her cheek, the bridge of her nose. "Some people aren't good at making relationships work."

"Some people means…?" She stopped as she saw such unhappiness in his eyes.

"Lara, my father is on marriage four. Before her death, my mother married three times. They were both good at making promises and lousy at keeping them."

That was the second time he'd mentioned promises broken. After witnessing his parents' inability to commit, she would guess that his own divorce had bothered him deeply. "Do you like his latest wife?" she asked.

"Never met her." His voice was quiet, cold. "You want to know why, don't you? Well, I haven't seen him in years, either. He was my biological father, nothing more. I don't know him. He doesn't know me. He's never even wanted to meet Joey."

How could someone who'd been raised by such a cold, unfeeling person be such a wonderful father? "His loss."

Beneath the darkness, his eyes held hers, urging caution. She realized what wasn't being said. He had no room in his heart for more than Joey. He wouldn't let there be more room in his heart for anyone except his son.

But she wasn't listening to the silent warning. Anticipation danced through her. She parted her lips, brought them close to his. A second passed before his mouth slanted across hers and took a deep taste.

Lara strained against him, her arms around his back. This was what she'd been waiting for again. What she'd found with him was special. Romantic words were sung about this kind of moment. People waited a lifetime for it. Her heart beat harder as she made a life-changing decision. She was going to have whatever she could have with him.

Heady with pleasure, she savored his taste. She felt his heartbeat. She wanted to be touched, to wrap herself in the taste and feel and smell of him.

She knew he wouldn't give her what she needed, but despite all the men she'd met, none of them measured up, none of them were him. Whether he was good for her or not didn't seem to matter. Fate or Cupid, or whatever force controlled an attraction, had chosen him for her and the feeling he stirred was unlike any other.

For a moment longer, Derek held her to him. "I should leave. Now," he insisted, but didn't let her go. The humor in his voice made her smile. "While I can."

It was only then she remembered she stood outside her building, that a few people were passing by. Tenderly she caressed his jaw, wanted to plead with him to stay. Instead, she leaned into him again, she kissed him hard but quickly, then turned away. For tonight let him think about that. She would.

She made nothing easy. With the warmth from her lips still on his mouth, Derek watched her rush up to the building's entrance. Greeting her, the doorman opened one of the double glass doors.

Until they closed behind her, Derek waited, watched. He'd tried to keep his distance, tried to forget the last kiss. He'd done a lousy job. She'd awakened needs and emotions he'd kept under control for three years. During that time, he'd had casual relations with a few other women, but what was driving him now insisted on more with her. He was complicating everything, and he damned himself because he didn't want to back off.

He wanted her, and she knew that now. The kiss had been too filled with a neediness that had grown since the last one. He'd ground his mouth against hers. He'd lapped up the taste of her, memorized the scent lingering on her skin. And none of it was enough.

With the blood pounding in his head, he'd struggled to back off. He'd been truthful with her. He would hurt her if he didn't back off. She deserved better than what he could offer. But when her lips had been on his, he'd wanted to forget everything except her and what she'd made him feel.

Lara had awakened before dawn with thoughts of him. She knew he could have had her last night. Breathless, wanting, she'd clung even when he'd begun to draw back. If she wanted to accept his terms, it would only be a matter of time, she believed.

Later that morning, at the center, she hadn't spent a moment alone with him. They'd both been too busy with patients to discuss anything but work. She didn't know if there was anything more to say. She knew his feelings, knew he didn't want to make a permanent place for her in his life. And she wanted so much more, she reminded herself. She would be wasting precious time with him. Frowning at her own ambivalence, she left one examining room. At the nurses' station, she found Derek on the phone.

"Rose, it's not a problem," he said. "I'll pick him up. Sure." She could hear the smile in his voice.

Lara liked that about him. He'd divorced this woman but had maintained an honest friendship. She looked back to see him glancing at his watch.

"Rose wants to stay at the hospital," he said. "One of her patients is in surgery. She was supposed to pick Joey up from a friend's place."

"Soon?"

"Forty minutes. I should be okay."

His eyes captured hers for a second. They could have been somewhere else, alone, caught in intimacy. "Yes," she murmured and forced herself back to the moment. "You have only one more appointment."

But he wasn't okay. As he left the examining room, he was unclipping his pager. "The hospital," he muttered as much to himself as Lara while he reached for the phone on the counter. "How far along?" Lara heard him ask. "I'll be there. Nine centimeters."

"Who?" Lara asked when he ended the conversation.

"Jeff Sawyer's patient, but he's out of town. I'll call Dorothy."

"Derek, I'll get Joey."

He was shrugging out of his lab coat. "Thanks, are you sure you don't mind?"

"I like being with him." She walked with him to the elevator while he scribbled down the address. "Do you want me to take him for something to eat before I take him home?" She stared at his bent head and itched to touch the thick, dark hair. She'd been sure she'd only thought that. But as he raised his head, she realized she'd placed two fingertips at the side of his neck.

He caught her hand, looked tempted to press his lips to her fingers. "About last night—"

"I wished you'd stayed."

A smile crept into his eyes. "Are you sure?"

"I'm sure." Lara inched back a step as a nurse came down the hallway. "I don't suppose a hot dog would be your idea of dinner for your son."

He laughed. "That would be Joey's idea of dinner. Hot dogs, spaghetti, pizza and macaroni and cheese are all he's willing to eat."

"Then we'll get a hot dog." It would have been so easy to stretch up for a kiss.

"He'd like that." He leaned closer but didn't touch her. "I really do owe you now."

She laughed, tried to make light of the moment, because a seriousness was grabbing hold within her. "What?"

His eyes came back to hers again. "Whatever you want."

Her pulse still drummed in her ears minutes after she'd left him, even though she was alone. He'd looked so serious. He wanted her, wasn't fighting this. And she knew exactly what she wanted.

Derek had made a phone call to inform the friend's parents that she was coming for his son. Picking up Joey was no problem. She truly liked being around him. "I need to go to my neighborhood before we head for your home," she told him.

A chatterbox, Joey talked nonstop. "We had lots of fun today playing with Adam's alligator game. I like them and dinosaurs and bugs best."

Was this how the bug man had started? Lara mused.

He sent her a solemn expression. "Girls don't like bugs."

"No, most girls don't. My sister had an ant farm."

His eyes brightened. "Cool. Does she have it now?"

"No, she's bigger. She's a mommy now."

As if they'd known each other for all his life, he linked his hand with hers. "Does she have babies?"

His question took her by surprise. This kind of moment was so like one she longed to have many times in her life. "My sister has a little girl almost as old as you." Lara tightened her hand on the small one. "And she has a baby."

"Babies pee a lot."

"I've heard that," Lara said, managing not to grin.

"Rylyn said storks don't bring babies. Her mommy said it must have been something in the water."

Lara chuckled. "In the water?"

"Where her mommy works, 'cause everyone is having a baby she said. Dorothy talked about bees when I asked her about babies.''

''What did your daddy say?''

''Babies grow inside mommies.'' He tipped his head questioningly. ''Who plants them there?''

Oh, boy. Keep it simple, Lara. ''God and daddies.''

He was silent for a long second. ''I'm going to grow worms if we get a house. Do you live in a house?''

Lara sighed with relief. Apparently they were done with the discussion about babies. ''No, I don't but that's okay. I really like where I live.''

''I do, too.''

''Do you like hot dogs?'' she asked when they neared a sidewalk vendor.

''Uh-huh. Naked.''

Lara dug into her shoulder bag for her wallet. ''One naked hot dog coming up.'' As he flashed that bright smile of his at her, Lara's chest filled with instant love. What a joy he was. That wasn't the smartest thinking, she knew. She shouldn't get too attached to him. While she could be hurt, get her heart broken, she needed to be careful for him, too. She didn't want to become too important in his life, then disappear, hurt him.

At Derek's home, they watched Joey's favorite dalmatian movie, had chocolate-chip ice cream and read a few books.

''Will you read another one now?''

"First a shower." Lara hustled him off toward the bathroom.

Minutes later he was wearing white pajamas with miniature black spiders on them. When he stood before her at the bathroom mirror, Lara tossed a towel over his dripping wet hair.

He giggled at her as she lifted the towel and spun around to see himself in the mirror. "Know what? Me and Mommy are going to visit Grandma Roseanne and Grandpa Joe before Mommy leaves on her trip. They live in Virginia."

Deliberately she matched his excited sound. "That should be fun." Obviously, Rose had done a fine job of explaining why she'd be gone.

"Lara, the phone is ringing."

She nodded, met his stare in the mirror. "It's for your daddy. I'll let the answering machine take it."

"Okay." He beamed at her. "Grandpa Joe has a dog. A mutt. That's what Grandpa Joe says," he added on a giggle. "I like my hair up."

"Up it is." She threaded fingers through the short, dark strands and spiked them up.

"Derek, it's Taylor," a sultry-sounding feminine voice said over the phone. "I've missed seeing you. Don't forget my little soirée on Saturday."

Lara frowned. Saturday was Danny's wedding day.

The woman purred. "My Park Avenue apartment. Please call. I'd love to see you before then."

No doubt, Lara thought. Was she someone from Derek's past or present? Regardless, she was someone

from his social circle, someone suitable. ''There you
are,'' she said to Joey. He looked adorable.

''Will you read the book now?''

''Hi, you two.''

In the mirror, she met Derek's stare. I missed you,
she wanted to say, but another woman suddenly appeared to have more of a right to say that.

Joey whirled around and jumped up into Derek's
arms. ''Daddy.''

''Hey, you're ready for bed.''

Wrapping arms around Derek's neck, and legs
around his waist, Joey pointed at Lara. ''We had
fun.''

Over Joey's head he mouthed a thank-you. Lara
returned a smile. He had no idea how much she'd
enjoyed herself.

Impatient, Joey tugged on Derek's arm. ''Can we
play one game before I go to bed?''

''We have time.''

''Yippee!'' He swiveled a look in Lara's direction.
''You, too?''

Lara saw an unusually wide grin on Joey's face.
Was five years old too young to start matchmaking?
She shook her head. ''No, I can't stay.'' She thought
they needed time alone before Joey left town.

''When will you read the end of that story you
started?'' Joey asked.

''I'll be back to finish the story. I promise.'' When
she crouched at his level, he threw his arms around
her neck.

''I had fun today.''

Lara's heart swelled. "Me, too," she whispered in his ear. "Me, too." Letting him go was harder than she'd expected. She started for the door. That's when she saw Derek's scowl. "Is something wrong?"

He stalled, saying nothing until Joey was out of hearing range. "How did it go tonight?"

I fell in love. "We had fun. He's hard to resist." She frowned because he was. "You look upset."

"Don't make promises to him."

She touched his arm, stopping him from turning away. "Derek, I will always keep that promise or any promise I make to Joey."

Something unreadable entered his eyes. "Promises aren't easy to keep."

"Not always." She couldn't go without having her say. With a hand on the doorknob, she paused and shifted her stance to look back at him. "I don't make ones that I won't keep."

Joey appeared beside him suddenly and smiled. "Bye, Lara."

Lara waved at him. A yearning within her grew even stronger. She wouldn't forget this day, this moment. Wittingly or not, both of these males held the promise of everything she wanted in life.

People didn't always get everything they wanted, she mused. She met Derek's frown with her own. They came from two different worlds. She'd already witnessed how impossible it was to blend them. "By the way, you have a message on your answering machine," she said as a reminder to herself that another woman existed. "Someone named Taylor."

Chapter Eight

Too quiet. No doors banging. No cartoon blasting away from the television. No small footsteps running down the hallway. Before Joey came back, Derek was certain he'd go crazy. He listened to the final hiss of his coffeemaker.

Since awakening, he'd been out of sorts. His son was gone, and the memory of a woman's kiss haunted him. Moving to the counter, he reached for the coffeepot. Earlier he'd turned on the radio. A romantic song about remembering drifted from it. A song meant to stir thoughts of a lover. Lara wasn't his lover, he reminded himself.

But every day she inched her way deeper under his skin. In the middle of the day, even when she wasn't around, he'd think about her smile, about the way her hair shone beneath sunlight, about how delicate her hands were. Three years he'd worked with her, three years he'd resisted these feelings. That hadn't been difficult at first. She'd been seeing the stockbroker then, and he'd nudged those thoughts about her aside. That had worked for a long time.

"Morning, Dr. Cross."

The click of the door swung him around and away from the coffeepot. "Dorothy, what are you doing here?" They'd agreed that she'd take some time off until Joey returned.

"I thought you might want company this first morning."

Sweet woman. "Thanks." He reached into a cupboard for another blue mug. Since the first day Dorothy had begun working for him four years ago, she'd been invaluable and had become a surrogate grandmother to Joey.

"Quiet, isn't it? He does make his share of noise around here," she said about Joey as she took a seat at the dark oak kitchen table.

Derek finished pouring coffee into the two mugs and set one in front of her.

"Will you be seeing her?" she asked after a cautious sip of the steaming brew.

"'Her' being…?"

"Joey told me all about her. Lara Mancini. Blond, tall, great at playing pinball, never been fishing. He's quite smitten. Are you?"

"This won't go anywhere with her."

"Maybe she doesn't want it to."

"She does." That's what worried him the most. Lara was lovely, caring and a willing friend and looking for husband material. He didn't want to hurt her.

"Think you might be wrong?"

"No." He shifted the conversation to Dorothy's favorite topic, politics. A loyal supporter of their mayor, she refused to believe Bill Harper would do anything to harm an establishment as fine as Manhattan Multiples. Derek wasn't so sure about the mayor. "If you're not busy today, stay." He poured them each another cup of coffee. "We'll watch the ball game."

She eyed his big-screen television. "Suits me."

Hours later, when the game ended, his stomach rumbled to remind him he hadn't eaten anything except the popcorn that he'd made. "Have a good week," Derek said as Dorothy was leaving.

On the way to the bedroom, he flicked off the television and grabbed his wallet from the top of the dresser. He jammed it into the back of his denims and headed for the door. He would like to claim that he didn't know why he suddenly had a craving for a pastrami on rye, but he'd be lying. Plain and simple, he hoped he'd see Lara at her neighborhood deli.

Lara went to the library, found a travel video about Switzerland and another about the Vikings and armed herself with three mysteries. She didn't know what might happen at the wedding. She didn't even know if she still had a date. Had Derek forgotten about a previous date with a woman named Taylor when he'd agreed to go to Danny's wedding?

Unsure if she'd be in a blue mood for the next few days, she deliberately lined up as many distractions as possible for the following day.

If Derek went with her, her family might prove too pushy at the wedding. He might feel she'd set him up. He was so commitment-shy that it was hard to know how he'd react to the Mancini clan. Well, she'd warned him, but who knew if they'd embarrass him in their eagerness to make him feel welcome.

If he went with her.

Feeling unsettled, she changed into jeans and a white gauzy blouse. With no destination in mind, she started walking. She needed people. Lots of people.

Turning a corner, she caught sight of Jodie stepping into Rosen's Deli. Even before Lara entered it, smells permeated the air—garlic, corned beef, spicy mustard, kosher pickles.

From a corner table Jodie waved to get her attention. "Your cell phone is off," she said when Lara was steps away.

Deliberately she'd left it off to avoid sisterly calls. Lara took a seat on a chair Neil pulled over from another table for her.

"We're having a party next week for Jeremy. You'll come?"

"Tell me when and where."

Distracted, Neil looked past her toward the door. "Well, this is interesting."

As all heads swung toward the entrance, Lara dealt with a nervous stomach.

"Who's he?" Casey asked with Derek's approach.

"Lara's doctor," Jodie informed her.

"Hmm." Casey propped her chin on her fist. "He could examine me anytime."

"Did you expect him, Lara?" Jodie asked.

Lara shook her head. Why had he come? To break their date?

"Hi," Neil said to Derek. "Want to join us?"

Jodie inched closer to him to make room for another chair at the table. "You can sit here."

If Derek noticed their studying looks, he gave no indication. He settled down close to Lara. Much too aware of him, of the heat of his body, she couldn't think of a thing to say.

"I was in the neighborhood."

Though he smiled, Lara strained for one. The purring voice she'd heard over his answering machine stuck in her brain. Had he come looking for her for a reason? "They have great food here."

"I remember you said that about this place."

Lara cast a look at friends, all wearing their oh-sure smirks. Before their interrogation started, Lara took control of conversation. "Have you talked to Joey?" she asked. "Is he having a good time?"

"He's in seventh heaven playing with his grandparents' dog."

"Who's Joey?" Casey asked.

"Joey's his son."

"If you're ready to order—" Derek said.

"I am." Lara ambled beside him to the counter. She was glad to get away from her friends' all-knowing grins for a moment, find out if he'd come looking for her to tell her he couldn't go to the wedding. Impatient by nature, she forced the issue. "About the message on your answering machine."

"I deleted it."

Emotion swirled inside her. "You deleted it?" She couldn't stop a smile.

Lightly he toyed with the chain of her gold necklace. "Pleased?"

"I thought you came to tell me you'd changed your mind."

"I came because I remembered the deli."

"So you had a craving for—"

The gentle hand on the back of her neck made her look up. "You. I had a craving for you," he whispered.

She let out a long breath, kept her eyes on him. Someone bumped her, she heard an "Excuse me," but all she saw was him.

"Lara," a gruff voice yelled.

Behind the counter, the deli owner insisted on her attention. "What do you and your friend want?"

Eating ranked second in her mind. She ordered her sandwich, but all she could think about was what he'd said. What woman wouldn't be thrilled by those whispered words?

"I'll carry these," Derek said about the baskets of food.

Back at the table, conversation shifted to Jeremy,

then jumped to some funnier moments in the life of an obstetrician before returning to their acting careers.

They ate and laughed, winding up the evening reliving a few humorous theater experiences, but more than once Derek's eyes met and held hers.

"Keep that date open for Jeremy's party," Jodie said when Lara stood to leave with Derek.

"I will." She exchanged goodbye hugs with each of them before joining Derek outside. A warm summer night's breeze greeted them. "I always have a great time with them."

As if it were the most natural thing in the world, he caught her hand. "Nice people." He looked down when her cell phone rang.

Lara knew she shouldn't have turned it on. As she groped in her shoulder bag for the phone, he stood closer, toyed with several strands of her hair. "I suppose ignoring it would be impossible."

He smiled with her. "I think so."

"Lara, they may need a substitute bridesmaid," her sister said without a greeting.

Lara looked up as Derek skimmed fingers down her arm. "Angie, that is not me."

"But you've done it before. You know what to do. How many times were you a—?"

"Six," Lara cut in. She rolled her eyes at Derek and mouthed "my sister." "I'm busy now, Angie. We'll talk tomorrow." After a quick goodbye, she dropped her phone back into her purse. "A family crisis. I'm being reminded that I've been a bridesmaid six times, so I shouldn't mind being one again. They forget an important fact. In our family, being a brides-maid that many times is a given. I have thirty-five cousins.''

''That's amazing.''

She managed a smile. ''I guess so.'' Would he stay tonight? Nervous from her own thoughts, she looked for more conversation. ''I'm surprised they weren't all in the wedding party. Danny's fiancée wants it all, the engraved matchbooks, though no one in the family smokes, napkins with their initials on them, exotic flowers in her bouquet, a reception at a hotel ball-room, and a honeymoon in the Bahamas. None of which he can afford, according to my aunt Isabelle, his mother.'' She shrugged. ''He loves Linda, so what else matters?''

''Does she love him?''

''No one doubts that she does. She simply wants a wedding to remember.'' As her hair fluttered beneath the breeze, she raised a hand to push back strands. ''But I'm not going to be in it.''

''I thought they had the wedding party chosen.''

At the entrance, Charley's night replacement nod-ded and held the door. ''They're not sure Rosa is going to be able to walk down the aisle,'' Lara added, and stepped into the elevator with him. ''She's having a difficult time.''

Was he going to stay? She couldn't think about anything else. Facing him, she curled her arms around his neck. She wouldn't forget that he'd said no strings, that there'd be no future with him, no mar-riage, no children. But long ago, her heart had opened to him. All she wanted to do was love him, if he'd let her. "You don't want to want me, do you?"

"I have no choice." He framed her face with his hands, held it still while his lips moved over it. "I realized that the moment I walked into the deli and saw you."

Wanting, she slid fingers along his neck to feel the texture of his skin beneath them. She wanted his touch. More. She'd have forgotten where they were if he hadn't.

Not letting her go, he urged her out of the elevator and to her door.

"You are staying, aren't you?"

"What a question." With a palm he slammed the apartment door shut behind him, then reached back to yank his shirt over his head.

She waited only until he'd tossed the shirt aside. Her pulse thudding harder, she took in a deep, quick breath. "I've been waiting for you."

He fingered the strings at the neckline of her blouse, untied it. "And you've made me ache since that first kiss."

Lightly she kissed a corner of his mouth, watched his eyes as he drew her blouse up. Take time. She wanted to go slow. Savor. But she felt no patience when he lifted her blouse over her head.

She sought the taste of his tongue, the warm recesses of his mouth. Her heart was filled with the excitement of the moment, with the neediness that had begun and blossomed within her since almost the first day she'd seen him. As the kiss deepened, a sweet pang of longing slithered through her. Emotion enveloped her. Her mouth clinging to his, she whimpered with his hand's descent over her breast to her hip.

Slowly he pushed the denim over her hips, down her legs. They nearly buckled when he kissed her belly above the black bikini panties. Her mind clung to the heat of his breath at her kneecap, his tongue at her ankle.

When he stood, she strained into him, kissed him again. This was what she'd wanted, him wanting her.

"Where?" he asked on a breath as harsh as her own.

Anywhere, she nearly said. She pointed, had no chance to say anything.

In one fluid move, he gathered her in his arms. Never had any man swept her off her feet. Her pulse racing, she whispered his name. She was so ready. In his arms, she felt the rightness of the moment and didn't want to think about anything else.

When he stepped into the moonlit room, she kept her eyes on him as he crossed to the bed. The steady, quickened beat of his heart pounded against her. The coolness of the room danced across her bare back.

His mouth clinging to hers, he lowered her to the mattress. Long and hard, he kissed her as if he needed the taste. Then, standing beside the bed, his eyes never leaving hers, he unzipped his jeans.

She wasn't a virgin, and as a nurse, she'd seen a man's body, but as she stared at him, strong and muscled in the shadowed light, her blood hummed. Her eyes moved down the broad chest, the flat rippled plane of his belly, the narrow waist and hips, to strong, sturdy thighs. And she knew he was ready, too.

Desire blossomed within her. She wanted to rush him, to feel the length of him against her, to know the fullness of him inside her. "You're a beautiful man."

On a low laugh he brought his face near hers. "You do that all the time."

Softly she moaned with his mouth's caress at the side of her neck. "What?"

"You make me laugh," he murmured.

"You make me—" She went silent when he hooked his thumbs in the waistband of her panties. "Sigh." She felt him roll down the wispy, black silk.

Naked before him now, vulnerable, she needed a touch—anything. "Kiss me."

Slowly he lowered himself to the bed and his mouth slanted across hers. "You're so beautiful," he whispered, pressing his length against her.

As flesh finally met flesh, she wrapped her arms around him. No more fantasy. All she'd been longing for was hers now. His mouth, hot against hers, ground hard with a greedy hunger. Breaths mingled, mouths tasted, passion heated. Need whipping through her, she skimmed fingers over his back, down the tight buttocks.

For a long moment, she drifted along on sensation. His hands caressed. His mouth seduced. Gently teasing, his lips traced a path along the line of her neck to her breast, stopped to taste first one nipple and then the other. His tongue continued its play, circled the pink bud, seeming intent on driving her mad with pleasure.

Each kiss he placed on her flesh, each moist caress of his tongue bound her even more to him. With excruciating slowness, his lips coursed down her body. She was past needing murmured promises.

When his mouth dipped lower, taunting her belly, she threaded fingers in his hair, held him close. She heard a soft moan, her own. Thinking had ended a second ago with his breath hot between her legs, his tongue stroking the core of her. She arched against him. Her skin damp, her heartbeat pounding with anticipation, she cried out with the pleasure of the moment. She'd known she would feel this way with him. She'd known he was the one.

Clinging a moment longer, she reached for breath, then moved. Took control. With her hands and mouth, she gave what she received, caressing, tasting his flesh, memorizing the hardness, the texture, his scent. These moments—these would be hers forever.

"Lara. Oh, Lara," he said, and gasped.

Bodies damp, they rolled until she was beneath him.

"You weaken me." He braced himself on his arms to rise above her.

She felt no patience as she took him in. "Derek—" Then she said no more. Without a word spoken, he filled her deeper. Her head went back, her eyes closed again.

Tightly she held him to her, wrapped arms and legs around him. For this moment he was hers. She answered the heat of his passion. She rocked with him, against him. She was his—unconditionally. It didn't matter what he offered. Her only thought was to give, to please him. She reached out as tension spiraled through her body. Linking fingers with his, she gripped his hand. He made her weak—and strong. He made her thoughts stop. Lost in him, she was his. Finally.

Minutes passed. Harsh breathing softened. Lara still clung to him. While her heart slowed to a normal pace, she had one coherent thought. Don't leave. She wanted him to stay, was afraid he'd flee now in the darkness. If he wasn't there in the daylight, he could deny to himself that they'd ever been together.

"You stun me," he said against her hair.

He sounded so surprised by his admittance, but she took comfort in words that declared feelings. Running her hands over his damp back, she wanted to keep him close even as he shifted to lift his weight from her. For tonight she didn't want to think too much.

Even in the dimly lit room, she saw an intensity in his gaze. He'd stay, she knew. They would make love again.

Drawing her close to his side, he waited for her head to settle on his chest, then he tightened his arm around her shoulder. "Give me a little while."

Amusement edged her voice. "And then?"

"Whatever you want," he said with a softness that made her feel caressed.

Happy, Lara curled into him. "Okay."

* * *

Darkness still mantled the room hours later. Derek lay in a jumble of sheets. For a brief second he considered moving, but the caress of her fingers across his chest stilled him. Shifting, he curled an arm around her shoulder to draw her closer. "You were wonderful."

"So were you," she said so softly that he barely heard her.

She'd given him so much, more than he'd expected. "You know I won't—"

Snuggling closer, she pressed fingertips to his lips to silence him.

This seemed so wrong. She'd given him so much, wanted so much, and he would give so little back to her. He wanted to be fair. He wanted to protect her, from him, but as she pressed her mouth against his chest, heat began to flow through him. Unable to think, he caressed her hair. His desire for her was all that mattered at this moment. When he touched the sharp point of her hip, she moved, sat on her knees.

Moonlight bathed her skin, cast a silvery sheen on her hair. In anticipation, his body quivered when her fingers seared his flesh. He stopped breathing, caught up in her, in the stroking caress of her hand.

He closed his eyes. Whatever they could have together, he welcomed. His heart racing, he let sensations whip through him. Breathless, he waited until choice no longer was his, then rolled her beneath him and let go of control. He led her and followed her. He journeyed with her once more. And he knew then that it wouldn't be enough.

Chapter Nine

At dawn he left. Lara took comfort in knowing that he seemed reluctant to let her go. Sitting on the edge of the bed, she smiled as she remembered last night. He'd come looking for her, hadn't he? There had been no other reason for him to show up at the deli. He'd wanted to find her. Then he'd made love with her.

He'd given her memories. She would never forget standing in her kitchen with the soft glow of daybreak brightening the room. They'd shared a few quiet, romantic moments while they'd sipped coffee at her kitchen table this morning. That time had carried as much intimacy as their lovemaking.

Reluctantly he'd pushed away from the table. ''I'll be back to pick you up for the wedding. Walk with me to the door.''

For a long moment he'd just held her.

She smiled now and roused herself from daydreaming, heard the trill of the phone. Family, she guessed.

"So who are you bringing?" Her sister Angie was on another fact-finding mission.

My lover. Just thinking the words warmed her. "My boss."

"You're dating your boss?"

She should have been prepared for this. "Angie, stop now. I didn't want to come alone. You know how everyone is."

"Oh, I do. So you're seeing this doctor?"

By her sister's response, she was totally unaware that she'd done what Lara was complaining about. "Tell me what dress you're wearing," Lara asked instead of answering.

"The lavender one with the lacy bodice. I don't look so hippy in it. What about you?"

Lara stood before her closet now. "I have no idea."

Her sister ticked off several dresses she remembered seeing in Lara's closet.

Lara assured her that she'd find something. But before she was ready several hours later, she'd tried on five different dresses. She decided on a black, slip dress with thin, glittery straps that stopped short of her knees. She drew her hair up and off her neck, then pulled a few tendrils free of the comb to frame her face. She slid on her black stiletto sandals, fastened dangling pearls at her ears, and snatched up her black clutch purse. She'd taken her time applying makeup, but she was still ready forty-five minutes early.

What if he was late? That wouldn't be his fault, she knew. Possibly she'd get a last-minute call from him, saying he couldn't make their date. She understood. As a doctor, especially an ob/gyn, his time was never his own. But her family would drill her with twenty questions if they were late or she came alone.

"I'm on time. Now there's a miracle," Derek said lightly.

She stood outside her building with him, looking beautiful with late-afternoon sunlight on her skin. Unlike earlier, her stare no longer held questions about them. Derek was glad because he had no answers. Lowering his head, he inhaled her scent, wanted to lose himself in her again.

As Charley discreetly gave a nod of what appeared to be approval, she smiled. "Did you have any trouble getting into the building?"

Derek guessed that the doorman's okay would please her. Everyone mattered to her. "The doorman was thorough."

"He asked a lot of questions before letting you in?"

"Just one." Derek slipped an arm around her waist and hailed a taxi, then glanced at her—again. The slip of a dress dipped low in front, drew his eyes to the faint shadow. As she stepped ahead, his gaze went to the low back and the expanse of flawless pale skin. His blood pounded. What normal male wouldn't feel his world rock when he looked at her? Amazing. He knew her body, had kissed practically every inch of it, and still his gut tightened at the sight of her.

"Derek."

By the tone of her voice, he guessed she'd asked him something. "What?"

"What question did Charley ask?"

"He asked if I'm a Yankee fan," he said against her hair. "I said I was."

"And he said?"

"Good." Unable to resist, he placed his lips against the velvety smooth skin at her shoulder. "Any guy who isn't a Yankee fan shouldn't bother to try."

She looked amused. "I'm almost afraid to ask. Shouldn't bother to try and do what?"

"Win your heart."

"Oh, my gosh." She made a face. "Expect more of that today."

"Am I in for it?"

"Definitely."

The church was crowded except for a few empty pews at the back. Wearing a lacy black shawl, Lara ambled with Derek to a pew near the front and an empty spot behind a man with salt-and-pepper hair and a pretty woman with dark-blond hair. "Let's sit there," Lara suggested.

In what her family would surely view as an affectionate and possessive move, Derek linked his fingers with hers. "Know them?"

"My parents." She tapped her father's shoulder. "Papa, Mama, this is Derek Cross."

A cheerful, outgoing man with smiling eyes, her father stood and pumped Derek's hand. "It's a pleasure."

Around her, Lara heard the buzz of voices, knew the family gossip had begun. Craning her neck, her aunt Millie nearly fell off the seat on a pew near the altar so she could see Derek.

Over her shoulder, her mother looked at them. "Roman's boy," she said about Lara's cousin's son, "balked about going down the aisle."

"Everything will be all right," Lara's father insisted.

"As you probably guessed, my mother worries about everyone and everything," Lara said low to Derek.

"They're nice together."

"After forty-three years, they understand each other."

He gave his head a small shake. "I've never known anyone who was married that long."

From what he'd told her, he'd witnessed his share of short-lived marriages. "Now for the rest of the family." Lara indicated her brother and his wife who were waving hands to get their attention. The whole Mancini clan was staring over their shoulders from their places several pews ahead. "That is my family," she said.

"Which ones?"

"All of them in those four pews."

At the sound of music, those in attendance turned their attention to the aisle, to the flower girl, Lara's sister Christina's five-year-old. In a sleeveless, purple taffeta dress, Rachel came down the aisle with the ring bearer.

"He's not going to do it," her mother whispered back to her about Roman's son, a four-year-old with flashing dark eyes, raven-colored hair and a dimpled smile. Today he scowled.

Halfway down the aisle, he halted and set the pillow down. He swung around and darted up the aisle toward the exit, dodging his mother's outstretched hand. Momentarily, soft laughter filled the church.

Smiling, Lara's father picked up the pillow with the rings and handed it to Rachel. "Carry the rings, too, sweetie."

Proudly she carried the ring pillow the rest of the way to the altar. Behind her, one by one, the pregnant bridesmaid brigade in purple satin came down the aisle. Elegant sprays of deep purple and burgundy and rose-colored blossoms concealed some of the round bellies. The matron of honor, Sophie, had gained five pounds in one week somehow. Her dress clung to her protruding stomach as she waddled down the aisle. She looked burdened but beautiful.

Linda was a radiant bride. A tall, slender brunette with a gleaming white smile, she wore white satin. Tiny pearls covered the bodice and the undersides of the long sleeves. Embroidered petals decorated the edge of the long, satin train. More pearls adorned the headpiece. Glowing, she broke into a smile the moment she saw her bridegroom.

At the altar, Danny, a fair-haired Italian like Lara, beamed. Lara loved weddings and never tired of hearing the vows. With Mancini flair, several bravos were yelled along with a loud round of applause when the happy couple was finally announced.

Inching their way with others to the bride and groom, Lara wasn't surprised Derek was stopped often by someone in her family.

Before they reached the huge ballroom of a nearby hotel for the reception, all of her brothers, sisters, in-laws, aunts, uncles, nieces, nephews and cousins had made their way to Derek.

"Could they wear name tags next time?" His fingers skimmed lightly up her back. "I'll never remember all of them."

"They don't expect you to." She smiled at him, realized she wished the evening was over, wanted to be alone with him again. "If you can remember one name, use it. They won't mind that it's the wrong name. They'll be pleased you remembered the one that you did."

Loverlike, he brought her close against his hip and urged her toward the doorman at the open door. "You're kidding?"

"No." She tilted her face up to his for a quick kiss. "We're a very congenial, easygoing group," she said, before briefly turning her attention to an ice sculpture of doves ascending from a basket.

Lara directed him to seats at one of her family's

tables. Across the room, the photographer snapped her camera. Roman's boy, smiling and happy now, even posed with Rachel.

The moment they sat down, her brother Mario cornered Derek into conversation about the World Series. "My sister is *the* number-one Yankee fan in the family."

"He knows," she said, not wanting Mario to go on about her.

He grinned and shifted the conversation from her to his pride and joy, a cherry-red Chevelle. Within minutes he and Derek acted as if they'd known each other all their lives.

Lara was relieved that he hadn't mentioned her unmarried state. Her relief was short-lived. Her aunt Isabelle, her father's oldest sister, a rotund woman with a propensity for large-flowered prints, stopped beside them and grabbed Lara's arm. "Is this your fiancé, Lara?"

Silently groaning, she avoided looking at Derek. But it wasn't as if she hadn't warned him about her family.

"He's her boyfriend," Millie, her father's other sister, piped in as she inched near.

"A friend," Lara insisted. "This is Dr. Derek Cross. My aunt—"

"A doctor!" Isabelle's eyes widened. "He's a doctor, Millie."

This was not going well. "My aunts." She gestured to one and then the other. Which one would describe her latest illness to him for a free diagnosis? "Isabelle and Millie."

Derek flashed a smile that was destined to weaken feminine legs. "Nice to meet you both."

"Handsome, Lara," Isabelle murmured in a stage whisper.

"Isabelle, come with me," Lara's mother said to distract her.

Lara dared a look at Derek. "I warned you. They're all certain that without their help I'll be without a man forever."

"Sit, sit," her aunt Connie said, materializing beside them.

"Make sure he eats," Millie insisted.

Lara rolled her eyes. "Trust me. No one will leave here without eating too much."

Dinner was both elegant and filled with the Old-World charm of a family feast on Sunday. Appetizers of shrimp in garlic sauce, proscuitto and crab puffs were followed by salad, then plates laden with prime rib and a chicken breast in bechamel sauce, side dishes of spaghetti and ravioli, crusty rolls, platters of cheese and fruit. Stories were recalled, dreams of the future shared. On the long table near the bride and groom was a three-tiered wedding cake, and an assortment of Italian cookies and pastries. Music began, adding to the festivities.

"You should dance," a voice said in Lara's ear.

Lara looked for a handy escape from her aunt Isabelle. "Can't. Sophie needs help with Cerra," she said, referring to her cousin's two-year-old.

"I'll go." Isabelle insisted, and she nudged Lara so hard at Derek that she plowed into him.

She kept her hand pressed against his chest. "Subtlety is not a family trait."

He wrapped an arm around her waist. "I'm not complaining," he assured her, pulling her even closer. "They're cute."

"Oh, you are a kind man."

"Come on, we'd better dance." Taking her hand, he led her onto the dance floor. As if she belonged in his arms, he gathered her to him. He had no idea how much his words meant to her. She could never love someone who didn't understand how important her family was to her.

For several songs they stayed on the dance floor, their bodies close and swaying to the melody. Lightly she curled her hand around the back of his neck and pressed her cheek to his. At the brush of his thigh, warmth rushed through her. She knew his body, the hardness, the muscles. It was as familiar to her as her own now.

"Quite a crew," he said of her family.

Did he find them overwhelming? She didn't doubt he'd gone to far more sedate and formal gatherings.

"I like them all," he said in her ear.

He warmed her with words that signaled he'd really enjoyed himself. With the last notes of a song, she scanned the room, spotted her aunt Isabelle talking to one of the band members. Lara abandoned her romantic daydreaming. "We should sit down now before—" She never finished what she planned to say.

Lively music suddenly filled the room.

"Have you ever done the tarantella?" she asked. Someone's arm hooked hers. Laughing, she grabbed Derek's arm. "You, too."

The good doctor proved to be a good sport. He looked down, tried to follow the steps, then, laughing, he backed off, hands up in a surrender gesture.

Dancing steps she'd learned as a child, Lara cast a sidelong glance at Derek. Beside him, her mother smiled and chattered. About what? Every embarrassing childhood folly she'd committed? Lara thought she needed to join them. "Are you having a good time?" she asked brightly to Derek after leaving the other dancers.

"Wonderful. Teresa shared the secret of her spaghetti sauce with me."

Teresa. Her mama must like him, to insist he call her by her first name. "Mama, you never tell anyone except family the secret of your spaghetti sauce."

"And good friends." She patted Derek's shoulder. "Now I have to find your papa." She kissed Lara's cheek to whisper in her ear. "Your doctor is nice. Papa said so, too."

Pleased, Lara sidled close to Derek and slid her arm around his back. "Did you learn I froze at my first dance recital?"

His eyes gleamed with amusement. "Did you?"

Lara winced. "Oh, Mama didn't tell you that?"

"No, she told me about her spaghetti sauce."

Lara moved with him toward the group gathering

around the wedding cake. Thank goodness. Family hadn't regaled him with stories of her youth.

His hand at her waist squeezed gently. "Only that you ran from a rooster at three?"

When she looked up, she saw the smile glimmering in his eyes. "You're a tease."

"A toast everyone," Mario announced from the other end of the reception hall.

More than one toast was made for the happy couple. Then came the announcement that the bride-groom would throw the garter. Several of Lara's cousins gathered near and nudged Derek and her onto the dance floor for the tossing of it and the bouquet.

Lara hung back, let a neighborhood friend's daughter catch the flowers. Derek sidestepped the thrown garter. Loudly Lara's aunt Millie moaned when her seventeen-year-old son caught it.

Amusement lingered while the bride and groom cut the cake.

"We can leave now," Lara said, assuming Derek had early-morning rounds at the hospital. "Or do you really want a taste?"

He bent his head, nibbled at her earlobe. "Yes."

Smiling, she drew him along with her.

Content. A moment passed before Derek registered where he was. He stretched his legs but they made no contact with the slim, warm ones his had tangled with during the night. Shifting from his side to his back, he turned his head toward the pillow, filled himself with the fragrant scent, her scent, that clung to it.

He missed her. He couldn't remember a moment in his life when he'd felt so content with any woman and so lost without her around.

Wrapping a hand around the brass headboard, he took the time to scan her sunlit bedroom. He remembered tossing the half-dozen brightly colored pillows in different shades of blue off the bed last night. He so rarely had a chance to laze around that he was tempted, but impatience nudged him.

He wanted to see her.

As he pushed back what he now knew was a hand-made quilt from Aunt Connie, a laugh tickled his throat. He'd never slept with a woman on cartoon character sheets. Scooby Doo was everywhere.

Still smiling, he yanked up his pants, and before leaving the bedroom, he flicked on the radio. The aria from *Madam Butterfly* drifted through the rooms.

Throughout the apartment, light flowed in from huge windows. He liked her home, including the movie posters, framed and hanging everywhere. In the living room, she'd added brightly colored throw pillows in blues to the white sectional. An expensive rug added color to the dining room with its plain, long, wood table that seemed more suitable for a farmhouse than Manhattan. He pushed in one of the white cane chairs.

Even before he finished going from room to room, he knew she was gone, made a logical assumption that she'd left for her shift at the hospital. He returned to the bedroom for the rest of his clothes. With his suit jacket in hand, he flicked off the radio, then wandered into the kitchen for the coffee she'd left him.

It was then he spotted her note: "Derek— Sorry I had to leave."

Smiling he took his coffee mug into the dining room. One wall was adorned with her family's photos. A day ago, they would have been strangers' faces. Now he could point and name most of the smiling people. In the past, getting close to anyone had never worked for him. He'd learned not to need anyone, anything. He'd learned promises were always broken.

His parents' legacy.

He supposed his father's phone call had stirred memories. He rinsed his empty mug and set it on the white drainboard. Through most of his childhood, his parents had been missing. Why his father was considering a visit baffled him. They had nothing to say to each other.

Turning, he stared at a calendar with cute photos of puppies that was pinned to a small cork bulletin board. Lara had scribbled in names to designate birthdays. Today's date bore a different notation. Dr. Kem—9:00 a.m.

A full second passed before his mind clicked with what he'd read. Gerald Kem was an ob/gyn. Damn. She was there for more tests. Why hadn't she told him? The last thing she needed was to be alone.

Lara had finished dressing. She felt sick with nausea from nerves despite Dr. Kem's assurances.

"Don't worry," he'd said, touching her shoulder before she'd left him.

If only that was possible. She strolled from the doctor's waiting room to the building's exit. She always understood patients' impatience when they had to wait for the results of lab work. She empathized with their anxiousness. The unknown was frightening. Managing a strained smile for the doctor's nurse, she said goodbye and opened the door.

That's when she saw Derek.

Standing on the sidewalk, he wore a frown. But he looked wonderful—unshaven, in last night's clothes. He hadn't gone home, hadn't showered, shaved, changed clothes. He'd forgotten everything except her. "Hi." She brought forth a smile. "Did you have the coffee?"

"I found it. And your note."

He'd come for her, to be with her when she'd needed him. Teetering on the edge of emotion, she worked for a calmness she didn't feel. "How did you know I was here?"

"The calendar. What did Gerald Kem say?"

She forced her brightest smile. "He has no answers, yet."

He held her close. "Don't expect the worst."

"Really, I'm not—"

"Don't. I know how you feel about family."

She gave in. Her heart felt heavy. No longer could she dodge the possibility that she'd have a life without a child of her own. "I wouldn't be the first woman who's never had children," she said with as much courage as she could muster. All she wanted to do was weep every time she allowed thoughts about never being a mother to grab hold.

Sometimes while she was holding a niece or nephew, pressure built in her chest. The urge to cry was always near. But long ago she'd decided the ache was worth it. She'd rather be with children than never have any of their laughter in her life.

"Lara." Catching her chin, he made her look up at him. "You need to remember something. I've seen women who have endometriosis, were told they'd never have children. A doctor isn't always able to give definitive answers about any patient.

Tears threatening, she looked down. "I know you're trying to make me feel better."

"No, it's more than that. A person is told they have an incurable disease, and against all odds, they live."

She knew he meant well. She, too, had heard about miracles.

"A woman with endometriosis came to me. She'd been told she could never have children."

"And she had a baby," she said, praying that he'd say those words, provide hope.

"No."

Lara drew a breath, wondering what point he was trying to make.

"She had twins. Even having endometriosis doesn't mean never."

"Stop worrying right?" she managed to say, but her throat felt tight. "I know you're right."

She knew, but keeping dismal thoughts at bay wasn't easy.

He waited for her to look up again, ran his hands down her arms, then as if he needed more contact, he gathered her to him. "I wish I could make this easier for you."

In a way, he was.

"Don't let this get you down."

"I'll try not to."

As his pager beeped he let her go. "Sorry."

Lara straightened her back. She needed to get ahold of the emotional seesaw she'd been on since leaving the doctor's office. Until the results were back, she didn't know if she was worrying needlessly. "You can use this," she said and withdrew her cell phone from her shoulder bag.

His voice went softer as if speaking more to himself than her. "I don't need it."

"But the page—"

"From my father."

He sounded so indifferent. There'd been no joy or anger in his voice. Tread carefully, she thought, wishing she understood him better. She waited, expecting him to say something, do something. Instead, head bent, he simply turned off the pager.

Chapter Ten

Derek sensed her confusion. As if she couldn't stop herself, she asked, "Aren't you going to call him back?"

He had no doubt that she would equate alienation from family with sadness. She'd never understand if he told her that he hadn't felt that kind of emotion since he was a boy.

"Derek, he is family."

"He's the man who produced the sperm."

Bafflement clouded her eyes. "When was the last time you saw him?"

He wanted to stop the conversation, not remember moments that had hurt him. "At my mother's funeral six years ago." Looking her way, he saw sympathy, a need to understand. To her, family and love went hand in hand. In their way, his parents had shown love—a pat on the head, a "good job" for becoming a doctor. But even those moments were rare. They'd given him everything he'd ever wanted, except themselves.

"He's never seen Joey?" she asked, pulling him from his thoughts.

"They had their own lives," he said with more sharpness than he'd wanted.

"Derek, family is important to you. Think about today. Tomorrow. Not the past." She angled her head to see him better. "You will call him, won't you?"

He gave her the answer she wanted. "Yes, I'll call. About dinner—"

"Dinner is my treat," she insisted.

That seemed best. He'd never invited any woman to spend the night at his home. There was always Joey to consider, and his home carried a message of more intimacy, more permanence.

Derek believed she couldn't understand about his father and him. Before she left, he saw a sadness for him still lingering in her eyes. He hadn't liked seeing it.

Unsettled, he headed home. She expected him to make the phone call. Why? What could his father want? Had his latest wife filed for divorce? Was he alone and had suddenly remembered he had a son and grandson? Was he ill? Derek searched his memory. He couldn't recall a day when Emerson Wentworth Cross had been ill.

He showered, shaved, dressed in a blue shirt he

knew Lara liked. Standing before the closet, he snatched a tie from a rack and moved to the mirror. He stared at a man who looked like his father when he was younger. Families shared more than looks, didn't they?

Snatching up the portable phone, he checked in his wallet for the phone number his father had left on his pager. It was for a first-class hotel in Manhattan. Four rings later, he left a message. The ball was back in his father's court.

He'd done his duty. He wasn't going to let thoughts about a meeting with him ruin his evening out with Lara.

At Manhattan Multiples, Lara was busy from the moment she walked in. She was still upset with herself. She'd gone too far, shouldn't have pushed Derek about his father. But he'd come to offer her comfort. All she'd wanted to do was return it to him.

She believed Derek was one of the walking wounded. Instead of bitterness or hostility, he'd spoken with indifference about his parents. Why?

She told herself that wasn't her business, but deep down, she ached for Derek, for all the times she sensed he'd been hurt, for the pain he might still feel.

"We're swamped today," Carrie said, breaking into her thoughts.

Lara nodded and rushed out for the next patient. Appointments filled the morning. Busy, too, Derek performed several prenatal diagnostic tests and an amniocentesis. Lara walked beside a woman who'd been tested for the presence of certain chromosome abnormalities and genetic defects including spinal bifidaes.

"I'm so relieved," the woman said, smiling.

"I'm glad for you." Lara went with her to the appointment desk, then returned to the examining room area.

She worked with a new patient, asking pertinent medical and family history questions. "Dr. Cross suggested an ultrasound to confirm the number of babies, heart rates and positions," Lara said, because she thought the woman needed explanations.

The woman clearly appeared upset, but said nothing to Lara about what troubled her. She seemed less anxious after Derek came in. Still the only sound in the room was the purr of the ultrasound machine.

Slowly he ran the sensor over her rounded stomach.

"When I had the first ultrasound, they located twins."

"Okay," he said, staring at the screen.

"When I went back for the next ultrasound—" She paused, glanced at the fuzzy image. "They only located one heartbeat."

Derek looked up in response to the sadness and anxiety in the woman's voice.

"I'm here because I'm hoping."

"Well, let's see."

Lara noted no concern in Derek's eyes.

"There's one," he said. "And two."

The woman's spirits lifted instantly. "Really? Two?"

"How about three? Would that make you happy?"

The woman's eyes widened as she stared at the image. "Are you sure?"

"Positive," he said, grinning at her. "They probably lined up." As he lifted the sensor, Lara wiped away the lubricating gel on the patient's belly. "You're definitely having triplets," he told the patient.

"She was stunned," Lara told Josie while they walked to a bagel shop for a light lunch.

"If she believed there was only one baby, why did she come to Manhattan Multiples?"

"Her sister said to see a specialist, be sure. She said she was hoping for multiples. Dr. Cross started her on vitamins, folic acid and iron supplements."

Grinning, Josie tipped her head questioningly. "Dr. Cross? Lara, I know the doctor is taking up a lot of your time these days."

"Everyone will know about us soon."

"Are you going to this week's fund-raiser together?"

"Yes. The small one at the restaurant." While wrapped in each other's arms, he'd mentioned it. "Derek is expected and—"

Josie sounded thrilled for her. "He invited you." Gleefully she rubbed her hands together. "This is getting interesting."

Derek used lunchtimes to read a few of the medical journals that were stacked on his credenza. Usually he liked the quiet, never minded being by himself. Today he missed Lara.

That wasn't the first time it had happened. Backing away from her wouldn't be so easy, he realized at that moment. The day would come. It had to. And deep down, he worried that she believed what they had might mean marriage someday.

He finished a gyro from a nearby Greek restaurant and tossed the bag into his wastebasket. He was pushing back his chair when the phone rang.

His hello was greeted by his father's stiff one. "You're not easy to contact, Derek."

"Do you have a problem?" He sat on the edge of the mahogany desk to look out the window with its view of Central Park.

"I was in town."

A second of wishful thinking invaded Derek's mind. He damned himself for wanting his father to say he'd come to see him.

"You're busy?"

"Usually."

Silence punctuated the strain between them.

"I'm not so young anymore," his father said, sounding as if it was something he just realized.

"Are you ill?" People didn't usually face their mortality unless illness visited them.

"No, I'm fine. I'm divorced again."

Derek nodded in confirmation to himself. He'd expected that. "Sorry."

"Don't be. I wasted years with her. I've done a lot

of years wasting time. When I was alone this time, it hit me that I hadn't seen you in—''

Derek didn't help him with an answer. He knew how long. They'd met one day for lunch years ago after he'd gotten his medical license, then again at his mother's funeral.

''I'd like to see you before I leave. Could you come to the hotel for a drink?''

How could he not ask about his grandson? ''Sure. What time?'' Derek agreed to the time his father suggested. He was glad that he wouldn't see him for a few days, needed the time to stop feeling angry. He had no reason for it, except he sensed his father hadn't changed.

Needing someone else, he left his office and strode a hall to find Lara. She was making a difference in his life. Just seeing her gentled his mood, he realized as he spotted her.

She flashed that million-dollar smile at him. ''Hi.''

He wished they were alone, wished he could pull her into his arms. ''I have one more appointment,'' he said to her. What he planned to say about dinner and a movie died on his tongue as his beeper went off.

He made several calls. His personal plan forgotten, and feeling rushed, he turned to leave for the hospital. ''Meet me at my place.'' He stepped near, pressed his key in her palm. ''You smell wonderful,'' he murmured for only her ears.

Her smile widened. ''I'll be there. Waiting.''

Lara stared at the key, tried not to make too much

of the gesture, but how could she not? Was he changing his mind about a short-term relationship, about no strings? Was that really possible? Or was his interest in her because she might not be able to have more children? She frowned at the key. What a thought.

Determined not to bring down her good mood, she spent the next few minutes planning a romantic evening. She stopped at the market, then headed home. She showered and changed into a silver-colored jumpsuit with spaghetti straps and matching sandaled heels. She grabbed a bluesy CD and a bag filled with the makings for dinner.

At Derek's, she was going to turn on music, but saw his collection leaned toward opera. She picked out an Andrea Bocelli CD to play during dinner. It wasn't difficult to locate a vase.

Smiling over how orderly he was, she easily found the right pots and pans, then took down ocean-blue plates, perfect dishware for her dinner.

"The Waterford is in that cabinet," a feminine voice said suddenly.

Lara swung around.

"I'm Dorothy."

"Lara," she said, and moved forward for the woman's hand.

Okay, he'd taken a big step by suggesting she come to his home. He'd made the decision to do—what? Make this relationship more than it was? He couldn't do that to Lara. He knew what a bad risk he was. He knew how miserable he could make her.

Softly he swore at himself. Tonight he'd make the break. He'd go in. He'd tell her they needed to call this quits—now—before the situation got complicated. That was simple, easy to do.

Nothing was simple, he realized a moment later. He opened the door, smelled wonderful aromas, heard music, then saw her dancing around the dining room table, a fork in her hand.

Trailing her was Dorothy, waving a spatula in the air. Two voices, a robust, sexy, musical one in tune, and a gruff feminine one that was slightly off-key were belting out an upbeat song about some guy's kiss.

Derek paused in the doorway and offered well-deserved applause.

Eyes wide, with a deer-in-the-headlights look, Dorothy tucked the spatula behind her back. Though still looking embarrassed, she recovered quickly and laughed. "Good night, Lara." She reached Derek at the doorway. "Dr. Cross."

As deadpan as he could manage, Derek held his hand out. "May I have your microphone?"

She laughed again and set the spatula on his palm. "I suppose you'll never let me hear the end of this."

He grinned back. "Never."

"What a great lady," Lara said when the door closed behind Dorothy.

"Sounds as if you were a hit, too." He thought she was unbelievable. He'd never known a woman who brightened a room so easily.

She craned her neck to see what was behind his

back. "Are those flowers for me-e-e?" she asked in a thick Southern drawl.

"For you."

"Ohh, I love purple irises," she said. "They're beautiful. Tell me." Her expression turned deadly serious. "Dr. Cross, are you trying to get me into bed?"

She looked stunning, slinky, seductive in the silver outfit that clung to her. No jewelry adorned the fabric. It followed the curve of her breasts, her waist, her hips. He found it enticing. "Is this working?"

She raised the flowers, inhaled their fragrance. Over the blossoms, her dark eyes sparkled with a smile at him. "Definitely."

"You look elegant—dazzling." He took her into his arms. "And something smells great."

"Shrimp stuffed with crabmeat."

"No," he whispered in her ear. "You do. I decided you owe me."

Leaning her body into his, she slanted a knowing look at him. "Owe you what?"

Lord, he wanted her. How was this possible? He'd thought that once they were together he wouldn't feel this way near her. But she was important to him.

Head back, she gave his lips room to explore her throat. "So what do I owe you?"

"Waking up together." He had missed that, wanted to be beside her during predawn light. "You cheated me."

"We'll have to fix that."

Idly he fingered the zipper at the vee of the jumpsuit. "My thought, too. Will that dinner keep?"

Drawing down the zipper he brushed a knuckle against her flesh above the lacy edge of her bra. "What a great invention."

Lara laughed. "Think so?"

"I love your laugh." The gnawing need for her surprised him. It went beyond a sexual need. "Your smile," he said honestly. "The smell of your skin."

Even as longing clawed at him, he checked his impatience. With a thumb, he nudged off first one and then the other thin strap from her shoulders. The shiny silvery cloth fell to the floor and pooled at her feet. All day he'd thought about her smile, even the sound of her voice. "I've missed you," he said against her hair, unable to keep the admission to himself.

"I missed you, too."

He strove for gentleness, but her mouth was on his, carrying a message that matched his own desperate need. Filling himself with her taste, he drew her down to the rug with him.

They'd made no promises, Derek reminded himself. She expected nothing from him. He wanted to cling to that thought, knew it was a lie. She would anticipate, yearn for so much more than he could give.

When she angled her head back to look at him, his gaze shifted to the creamy flesh above the wispy black bra. He'd been with her and still ached for the feel of silky flesh beneath his touch, the sweetness of her mouth, the heat of her sigh against his lips.

He'd forgotten to keep everything simple, to keep the relationship free of strings. Without doing anything, she pulled at him. She made him want more even when he tried to need less.

Skimming her flesh, memorizing the curves and angles, he drew silky material from her hips, followed a trail to her upper thigh, tasting where he'd caressed. He had one goal. To please her.

Beneath his touch, her body heated. Beneath his mouth, her skin quivered. His pulse pounding, he shifted his body so he could see her eyes. In the shadowy darkness of the room, they looked so soft, so trusting.

He'd do his best not to hurt her. He made the silent promise. With passion clawing at him, he buried his face against the side of her neck and lifted her hips to him.

Already lost in her, he whirled beneath sensation as he entered her. With a moan, he felt a fiery rush dance over him. Hot, damp, they strained against each other. And he prepared for the madness again, the madness that would give him serenity.

Less than a few hours ago, what had he planned to say? He had no words now, Derek realized. He didn't even understand when he'd lost control. She made him want more than he'd ever wanted, love—promises. Far-fetched possibilities. In his family, promises weren't kept. He wouldn't make them to her, any of them.

He shifted, took a deep calming breath, then raised himself up on his arms to relieve her of his weight.

''Don't leave.'' Her words came out on a whisper.

He chuckled. "Leave? I can barely move."

Laughing, she coiled her arms around his neck. "Then don't."

He stayed, served her coffee and fruit in bed, made her laugh when he fed her pieces of cut apple, the only fruit he had in the kitchen.

Her laughter bubbled out again and rippled on the air when he threw her over his shoulder and took her into the shower with him.

Fun. She'd had fun. During the lighthearted morning, they'd laughed like teenagers totally infatuated with each other.

Standing in her kitchen, Lara recalled every second. With the notes of a bluesy saxophone wafting on the air through the sunny room, she chopped a green pepper for an omelette.

In the middle of the kitchen table stood the vase of flowers he'd brought her. She'd never expected him to bring her flowers, to romance her. In all the time she'd been with him, had a crush on him, she'd never expected that he possessed a romantic streak. Never had she thought that one day he'd take her hand or kiss her, much less be the man in her life.

She smiled at the flowers again. She'd keep them forever, she knew. When the stems no longer stood straight, she'd press the wilted blossoms between pages of a book and treasure them forever.

"So what goes into an omelette in the Mancini household?"

Lara glanced away from chopping the green pepper. Unshaven, his hair tousled, he looked sexy to her. "Anything you want in it." Head bent, he stood bathed in morning sunlight at the kitchen doorway while he buttoned his shirt. "What do you like?" she asked. "Onions, green peppers, mushrooms, cheese, tomatoes?"

"Okay." He stepped up close behind her, placed a hand on her belly.

"You're incredibly easy to please."

"I'm feeling mellow."

"I wonder why."

Gently he nibbled at her ear. "I can't imagine."

He did look tranquil, satisfied, she thought, watching as he straddled a kitchen chair. "You have a message," she said with a nod at the answering machine.

"Nothing urgent."

Because his beeper received hospital emergencies, he wouldn't be concerned. But Lara couldn't help asking, "Aren't you curious?"

He laughed and stretched an arm out to hear the message. "Are you one of those people who'll break a leg jumping over furniture to answer a phone?"

"'Fraid so," Lara admitted. "I also shook Christmas presents when I was young."

Smiling, he pushed the button.

"Derek, it's your father. It seems we'll be playing phone tag again. I've taken a room closer to your office."

Lara slanted a look at him.

Staring at the floor, he listened to the phone number his father had left but didn't write it down.

"Are you going to see him?" she asked.

Annoyance furrowed his brow. "Why do you care?"

"Because you do."

"I don't." He leveled a cool, unemotional expression at her that was meant to end the discussion. "That's what you don't understand."

She might have stopped if she'd believed him. Sometimes the person denying something was the last person to learn the truth. "Tell me why." She couldn't stand the bitterness she'd heard in his voice. "You said that your parents divorced. When you were young?"

"Eight." He looked as if he wondered how they'd begun to discuss his family.

Lara knew he wanted her to stop; she couldn't. "That must have been difficult for everyone."

"My parents married to merge two influential families, not because of love. When they divorced, they fought for custody of me, fought to make each other miserable. But neither of them wanted me."

Lara doubted that. Young children sometimes saw situations differently from the way they really were. "How can you be sure of that?"

"He lost the custody battle and went to Jamaica with the latest girlfriend."

Lara heard that cold indifference in his voice again. "That doesn't mean—"

"She won custody and shipped me off to boarding school."

Lara ached to put her arms around him, but knew

better than to offer comfort. He'd give, but never accept it.

"I can't recall them being at one tennis match to watch me play or one school activity. They weren't there for birthdays or Christmas. They weren't meant to be parents, didn't want to be. They had their own lives. I was a necessity to carry on the family name."

Her heart twisted for the boy who'd gone without love. "I'd call, ask if they'd pick me up for the holidays. 'I'll be there,' they'd each promise, and neither of them showed up."

A heaviness began to settle in her chest. They weren't talking about this strong man. They were talking about a little boy, waiting, expecting, longing to see his mommy or daddy. They'd let him down. They'd done something no parent should do to a child. They'd left him without someone to trust. He'd never been able to depend on the people he should have been able to trust the most.

"Don't look like that," he appealed. "I'm not telling you this for sympathy. I want you to understand I meant nothing to them. And I know what divorce does to a child."

Wanting no distraction, she turned off the stove burner. He wasn't talking about his parents now. He was talking about his divorce. "But you and Dr. Clayson have a good relationship."

"We've always thought of Joey first." He scowled. "At least, she had in the past."

Her head spun from how quickly he shifted their conversation away from him. With little choice, she followed his lead. "Derek, she won't be gone for long, will she?" During the past three years, she'd gathered the impression that he was proud of his ex-wife's accomplishments. What was really bothering him so much?

"What if I let him down?" he asked, meeting her stare.

"How could you let him down?" Though confused, she thought it important she understand. "You're not leaving."

"No, I'm staying." He moved to a window, offered his back to her. "But I'm an obstetrician. You more than anyone should know I can never plan anything."

"That's true, but—"

He pivoted around, faced her. "Rose won't be here. And I won't, either."

"Of course you will."

"No, I won't. He'll be at a baseball game or a school assembly, and like every other kid, he'll look in the audience for his parents. His mother won't be there. What guarantee is there that I'll be there for him?"

Desperately she wanted to ease his mind. "Derek, that won't happen—"

He sliced a hand in the air to cut her off. "It shouldn't ever happen. It's not fair to him. He deserves to feel that someone wants to be with him more than anywhere else."

You, too. He knew that heartbreak, she realized. "Derek, if that ever happens, I'll be there. And you said Dorothy really loves him. I'll call Dorothy. We'll both be there.''

"You'll be there?"

"I promise."

His lips curved in a humorless smile. "That's a nice gesture, Lara, but you could be living somewhere else, have a family of your own to worry about."

His words cut through her, shattered an illusion she'd had about him beginning to have feelings for her. She'd fallen in love with him, had hoped that he and Joey would be a threesome with her. He'd just told her differently. That fantasy would never happen.

"You can't guarantee anything, Lara."

She struggled with emotions, not willing to let him see how much those words hurt her. "No, I can't," she admitted because she had no choice. Still she refused to let him go on believing that he'd let Joey down. "But I do know that if you're not there, Joey will understand."

"You don't know that."

"Yes, I do," Lara insisted. "He'll understand because he knows how much you love him."

"You really believe that, don't you?"

"How can you not?" Sometimes she wanted to cry for him. "Sometimes you have to have faith in another person. You've given him no reason not to believe in you." Even as she said the words to him, she knew he didn't believe her.

He settled at the table again, picked up his coffee cup. "I don't want to talk about this anymore."

Just like that. She heard such finality in his voice.

He'd closed the door again, she realized. Family meant different things to them. Unlike him, she'd always known people who cared about her.

"What do you want to do today?"

"Anything. Or we could do nothing," she said. "I bet you don't laze around often."

"Hardly ever." As if needing closeness, he caught her wrist and drew her down to his lap. "But we'll think of something."

Chapter Eleven

The distinguished Dr. Cross in-line skated. No one was more surprised than Lara.

"Joey," he said simply as an explanation before they headed out of Central Park. They'd skated, holding hands, then had eaten hot dogs. One wonderful day turned into two, then a weekend. She ran in the park with him in the morning, took a carriage ride at night. Everything they did was right out of some fantasy she'd had over the years about being with him. The next few days included a night at the movies, simply staying at her place and watching television and sitting outside with a caffe latte and reading the newspaper.

When Joey returned, she sensed Derek would back off. He wouldn't want his son getting attached to her, but for now she had almost everything she'd ever wanted.

"Here's your ice cream." He stepped close and handed her the cone.

"You're not having any?" she asked while they strolled along the sidewalk in Central Park.

He shook his head. "When do you go back to the doctor's?"

"At the end of the week." She offered the cone to him. "Have some," she said. At the sound of children's laughter as they chased each other around a park bench, she frowned.

"Lara—"

She licked harder at the ice cream he'd just bought her. "Let's not talk about that." She wanted nothing to spoil their time together.

But his hand cupped the back of her neck, forcing her to look his way. The look in his eyes nearly undid her. "We all carry emotional baggage, Derek. This isn't a new problem for me." Still whenever she thought about it, her heart cracked a little more. "Years ago I was told I might have trouble getting pregnant. But the possibility of endometriosis wasn't diagnosed. Most men want a child to carry on their name. You have Joey."

"We're not talking about me."

She pivoted away to avoid his stare, certain she'd give in to self-pity if he gave too much understanding. "About tonight's party for Jeremy— Jodie said to come anytime after eight. People will breeze in and out."

"Big party?" he asked.

"Oh, no one ever knows. Ten, thirty, a hundred."

He followed her lead to lighten the mood. "You're kidding, aren't you?"

"No. People drop in. You'll see. There's a ball game on television today," she said, changing subjects. "You *are* going to invite me over to watch the end of it, aren't you?"

He slipped an arm around her waist and tugged her close. "So, you're seeing me because I have a bigger television."

Grateful for his tease, she smiled and stretched up for a kiss. "Bigger bed, too."

At nine o'clock, they were climbing steps to a studio apartment in West Village. The party overflowed. While some people milled about in the hallway, others, deep in conversation, lingered on the stairway. Her hand in Derek's, Lara led the way up the stairs and around other partygoers.

Music, a raucous rock 'n' roll song, greeted them, steps from the door. "There's Jeremy," Lara said, seeing her friend surrounded by a small group.

Lara didn't have to introduce Derek. People she'd known for years rushed forward to say hi and introduce themselves. Lara expected the response. Theater people were used to new faces, and quickly made friendships.

While Neil urged Derek to join him at the makeshift bar, Lara spotted Gena across the room and made her way to her.

Her friend looked lovely, relaxed, smiling. The last time Lara had seen Gena she'd been depressed. Lara hugged her, then held her at arms' length. "You look absolutely wonderful."

"Probably because I'm pregnant."

"You're what!"

"Pregnant," Gena practically screeched.

"Oh, my gosh. Oh, my gosh." Lara grabbed her, hugged her hard. "Gena, that's wonderful. I think I'm going to cry." She drew back, searched her face. "You are glowing."

Her friend beamed. "Inside, too."

"How?" Lara asked.

"You're a nurse," she teased. "You know how it's done."

"No, I mean—"

"I know what you mean," Gena said more seriously. "I was due for a hysterectomy next week. And here I am pregnant. It's a miracle for Tony and me. The doctor said the pregnancy should help with the endometriosis."

"I was so upset for you when you told me about the hysterectomy." Lara drew a hard breath, but tears stung her eyes. "And now I'm so happy for you."

"Thank you. I know you are." Shifting her stance, she eyed Derek. "Enough about me. Tell me about him," she said with a subtle nod in Derek's direction. "It's the boss, isn't it?"

"Yes."

"Are you two serious?"

"It's nothing like that. I told you. He's wary of involvement, Gena."

"But he's with you. And I know how you are." Gena slid an arm around her shoulder. "You never give up. That's your best trait."

Lara wanted to believe in her and Derek, wanted to believe she would receive good news at the doctor's, but it was hard to keep her spirits up. "Come on. You need to meet him."

Gena strolled arm in arm with her toward Derek. After Lara introduced them and shared her happy news, Gena said, "I'll call, and the two of you can come over some night for dinner."

Lara smiled. "I'd like that." But she knew making long-term plans for her and Derek wasn't smart. "I'm so happy for her," she said to him once they were alone.

"That should be a good enough reason for you not to worry about your test results. Things aren't always the way they seem."

"Yes," she said. "But miracles don't happen every day." Sipping the wine in her glass, she scanned the sea of faces. "Are you having a good time?"

He skimmed fingers down her arm. "I like being with you."

"I know," she said meaningfully.

"No, I don't mean that way. I like being with you even doing nothing."

That's love, she wanted to say, but doubted he'd believe her. She wanted to cling to his words, knew better. "We could mingle a few more minutes. And then—"

"It'll be fun."

Head back, she laughed up at him.

He pressed his mouth to her temple. "Lots of fun."

Early-morning sunlight bathed the bathroom. Derek raised his face to the water spraying at him in the shower. He admired her courage. She'd worn a brave face last night. He didn't doubt her happiness for her friend was genuine, but worry for herself must have hampered some of the joy for Gena. Lara deserved what she longed for most.

Grabbing the bar of soap, he let the water rush over him, listened to the radio blasting away. In the kitchen, wearing his robe, she'd been singing away with Rod Stewart before he'd left for his shower. It felt right to have her in his home, in his kitchen, in his robe.

All last night he warned himself, but he couldn't seem to stop wanting to be with her. Even the talk about a pregnancy hadn't disturbed him as much as it might have.

"Company's coming," a voice sang out to him a second before the shower door opened.

In one swift move, he caught her at the waist and pulled her in. This is what she brought into his life. Spontaneity, laughter, fun. "Come here." She giggled when he cupped a hand around the back of her neck and drew her under the water with him. Skin touched—breast to chest, belly to belly, thigh to thigh.

On a sigh, her head fell back and she closed her eyes as his soapy hand moved up and down and over her outer thigh.

''Want some?'' he murmured against her slick collarbone.

She released a soft giggle. ''What?''

''Soap.'' He set the white bar in her upturned palm.

''Did you soap this yet?'' she asked, rubbing it down his back.

''Not yet.''

Her lips trailed over his jaw. ''What about here?'' she asked and ran the slippery bar along his groin.

He took a breath. With a kiss or a caress, she could make him forget everything.

Smiling, she slanted a look his way. ''Or here?'' she murmured. The soap thudded on the floor.

As her hand closed over him, a groan stirred in his throat. Sensation ruled. He shut his eyes, gave his body to her. Effortlessly she had the ability to drive him crazy, take him beyond thinking, beyond reasoning.

In seconds, he was breathing hard, swamped by sensation. He swung around, turning her with him and pressing her against the wall of the shower. Water sprayed over them as he gripped her buttocks and lifted her to him. Her legs tightened around his waist as he entered her. Steam rose around them. Each thrust bound them more. With the water beating at his back, his gaze met hers. Her eyes were filled with emotion. And for a brief moment all he cared about was that she was his.

Love. Lara knew she'd never really been in love. The time with James had been a passing thing. Love felt different. A sense of rightness filled her just because Derek was near. Still she hadn't met his father or his friends. She thought the fund-raiser, an event more in line with his social life than hers, might emphasize just the opposite—how wrong they were for each other.

While Derek left to make rounds at the hospital, Lara had gone home to change before heading to Manhattan Multiples.

By nine, she was approaching the building's entrance. She zig-zagged her way between the crowd hustling by, and saw a woman standing still, flattened against the building as if glued to the exterior. Blond, slender, petite, in her late twenties, she was very pregnant. By the way she was dressed in an oversize, faded, print top over faded jeans, she was going through hard times.

A few steps from the woman, Lara made eye contact and offered a smile. "I'm a nurse here. Were you waiting to go in?"

Uncertainty edged the woman's voice. "Sort of." Her chin tucked in, she still hadn't looked up.

Lara reached out but didn't touch her. "Why don't we go into the building and away from the crowd."

With the woman's movement away from the wall, Lara had a full view of the left side of her face. Blue, black and a touch of green discoloration marred the woman's smooth complexion beneath the eye and over the cheekbone.

Schooled in seeing disturbing sights, Lara veiled any reaction and held the door open for her. "You're in the third trimester?" Lara asked as the woman passed her.

"Yes."

Shy? Or wary? Lara wasn't certain why the woman was so apprehensive. Perhaps she simply had learned not to trust anyone. Taking it slow, Lara waited until they were in the elevator before asking, "Are you having multiples?"

The woman stayed against the back wall. "A doctor told me he thought he heard three heartbeats. I was told that the doctors here see mothers who are having more than one baby."

Lara's concern grew. She waited while the woman preceded her out of the elevator. Had the woman been taking prenatal vitamins? Had she had any doctor's appointment during the past months? "Are you new in the city?" she asked.

"No, I've been here for a while. I'm from St. Louis."

As the elevator doors swooshed open, Lara spotted Derek. The sooner this woman saw a doctor, the better. "Dr. Cross," she called out to get his attention.

When he glanced their way, he maintained a friendly smile even though Lara had seen his gaze flick to the woman's bruise. Lara made the introduction. "Mrs. Simpson believes she's carrying triplets."

"That's wonderful."

Though the woman might be destitute, she reacted as they'd hoped. "Yes, I was shocked." She beamed. "I never expected more than one baby."

Derek took control. "Eloise Vale is the center's owner. She likes to meet all of the mothers-to-be who come in here."

That was true, but Eloise didn't always meet them before the first examination. Derek obviously felt he needed to involve her immediately. Chances were that Leah Simpson had no health insurance.

"Let me call her. Then we can go downstairs to her office." Derek ushered her to a waiting room of chairs. Walking away from her, he discreetly signaled Lara to join him at the appointment counter. "Find out about the bruises," he urged Lara when he was reaching for the phone.

Lara returned to the waiting room to sit beside Leah Simpson. "Manhattan Multiples provides the best of care for mothers and their babies. How did you learn about the center?"

"There was a doctor at the emergency room. He told me where the center was."

Lara looked up from jotting down the information. "Did you have to go into the emergency room for the babies?"

"Something else."

She had to ask. "Was the something else that?" she asked, touching her own face near the eye.

"Not this time. A few weeks ago. I had a really

bad headache this time, but didn't want to take anything because of the babies.''

Lara couldn't let her go back to the man. Four lives depended on the right decision now. ''We could call the police.''

''No.'' She shook her head adamantly. ''No police.''

Intensifying the woman's humiliation wasn't her goal, but she couldn't back off. Domestic violence against women sometimes became worse during pregnancy. ''Do you have concern for your personal safety?''

She shrugged. ''He gets mad sometimes.''

Lara wanted to know if ''he'' was a husband. ''Does he get angry often?'' she asked because that question was more important.

''It's okay now. I left him.''

Hoping the woman was telling the truth, Lara gave her hand an encouraging squeeze. At the sound of footsteps, she looked over her shoulder.

Derek ambled toward them. ''Mrs. Simpson, if you come with me, we'll see Eloise and then we can talk about your medical care.''

''You're being nice. But—'' She looked uncomfortable.

Derek hurried his words to save her pride. ''Your care and the care of your babies is our main concern. Don't worry about anything else.''

Those were exactly the words that the woman needed to hear. It always amazed Lara that he'd come from such a cold, uncaring home when he had such a compassionate nature.

"Lara, Mrs. Simpson is going to have an ultrasound."

"I'll take care of preparations."

"After you're dressed, you'll go back to Eloise's office," Derek reminded her.

"Okay." Her frown remained until her ultrasound. A look of awe swept over her face while she stared at the snowy images of her babies. "That's them?"

"That's them," Derek said.

Slowly a smile filled with joy settled on Leah Simpson's face. Something close to hero worship sparkled in the woman's eyes. "Thank you." She clutched Derek's hand between her own. "Thank you so much."

Pleased at how things were developing for the woman, Lara left the room to get vitals on another patient. Aware Derek had a few minutes before he needed to be in another examining room, she headed into his office. She found him leaning against the edge of the mahogany desk and studying a patient's chart. "You are so good with people," she said, and stepped into the space between his spread legs.

Not looking away from her, he set down the chart to place his hands at her waist. A seriousness remained in his eyes despite the smile that came to his lips. "Don't expect too much from me."

Lara considered his words of caution. They were too late. While she expected nothing from him, she couldn't stop longing for everything.

"Meet me at my place."

"It's a date," she said brightly, feeling as if nothing could ever go wrong. Before she hurried from the room to usher in the next patient, she heard his phone ring.

Pleasure warmed his voice. "Hey, Joey."

His son. He'd given Joey everything he'd never received. And she sensed that in his way, he was afraid to believe or trust in the love of anyone except his son.

"Daddy, Grandpa Joe said Buster's going to be a daddy," Joey said about the family dog.

Derek mentally geared up for his son's next words.

"We could have a puppy, couldn't we? We're allowed. Mrs. Loman has a dog," he said.

Mrs. Loman, a neighbor, had a Pekingese named Chauncey. "Joey, Buster's a golden retriever."

"I know." Joy filled his voice. "He's so cool."

And big, Derek recalled.

"If you throw a ball, he jumps in the air to catch it, and he does lots of things. Can't we have a puppy?"

"Puppies become dogs. You have to walk them and feed them and—"

"I know, Daddy. I will. I promise."

"Joey, we'll talk about it after. There aren't any puppies yet, are there?"

"No. But Grandpa Joe said there probably will be because Buster and Cleo—that's his neighbor's dog, she's a Lab-Labrador—were making babies. Daddy, can I call Lara when I get home?''

Derek switched mental gears to keep pace with him.

"Do you know her phone number, Dad?"

"Why?" he asked, instead of answering.

"I want to know when she's coming over."

Derek wanted to say no, but Joey wasn't asking permission. He assumed she'd come. The question was when. "Is Mommy there?" Derek asked.

"She's right here. Daddy wants to talk to you."

"Rose?"

She was laughing. "I just knew you'd have a fit."

"Did he see the dogs?"

"Only for a second. He wasn't aware. He thought they were playing. Worried about doing the birds-and-the-bees talk?"

"He does seem obsessed with how babies are made."

"That's not surprising, since both his parents deal with babies."

"Well, you're the pediatrician, the expert. You tell him."

She laughed. "I thought you already did."

"Not enough, I guess." Derek couldn't help smiling. About Joey. And just because, he realized. That's what Lara did to him. She made him feel good, want to smile. She made him laugh at himself, relax. She made him enjoy life.

Well after sunset, Lara met him at his home. Standing beside Derek while they chopped vegetables, she was finally able to satisfy her curiosity about Leah Simpson. "What did you learn about her?" she asked, and set the broccoli on a plate with onions for the stir fry.

Derek paused in chopping carrots. "She's homeless."

"Oh, that's terrible," Lara said, though she'd gotten that impression.

"Eloise is temporarily taking care of that situation."

"And the bruises? Mrs. Simpson admitted to me that she had to go to emergency. More than once for beatings."

Lara went to the refrigerator, removed celery stalks from the vegetable crisper. "She also said she was estranged from her husband now."

Setting down his knife, Derek glanced up. "She doesn't think he knows where she is."

"Good." Lara chopped off a slice of celery harder than necessary. "I hope she won't go back to him," she said, opening the silverware drawer.

"The last time, he punched her in the stomach."

As she considered how dangerous that could have been for the babies, she drew a quick breath.

"Lara." He cleared the chopped carrots off the cutting board and into a bowl. "Tomorrow evening—"

Why would he bring up the fund-raiser dinner now? "What about it?" Tense, she made herself ask, "Have you changed your mind?"

"Not me." He raised his head and gave her an easy smile. "Have you?"

She'd planned to buy a new dress, had anticipated the evening out. "No." Was there a problem? She couldn't imagine what it could be.

"You know they'll be plenty of gossip about us after tomorrow evening."

Was he really worried what people he knew would say? James had always been terribly preoccupied with others' opinions. "I don't care."

"You don't?" With the shake of her head, he smiled again. "Ah, yes," he teased. "You're fearless."

She'd never been a fearful person. She used to watch horror movies when her cousins and siblings hid behind chairs.

"Don't be too brave," he urged.

This was about them, then? Lara realized. Was he hoping she'd back out? "I'd rather feel and take chances than never feel anything."

He arched a brow. "You think I don't?"

"I think you try hard not to love."

"You should try harder," he said, and drew her into his arms. "I told you once not to expect too much. I can't give as much as you."

Too late, she thought, and struggled to block tears as a pressure in her throat threatened to snatch breath from her. Too late.

Chapter Twelve

Since childhood Lara had proven stubborn when she made her mind up about anything. She didn't argue with Derek, didn't want to spoil the rest of their day together.

By midafternoon they settled on the sofa to watch a ball game. She decided the baseball game definitely looked better on his television than on her twenty-one-inch set. "I think I'll put a big-screen television on my wish list."

He waited for her to set down her knitting, then handed her a glass of wine. "You have a wish list?"

"Everyone does." As he plopped on the sofa beside her, she elbowed him. "You do, too. Come on. What would you like that you don't have?"

"An airplane." He smiled as if amused by a private thought. "When I could have it, I didn't have the money to buy it."

"Derek, you come from money."

"Not family money. My money." He set an arm on the cushion behind her. "I don't use the family money. It's there for Joey someday if he wants it. I don't," he said in a voice that carried a trace of bitterness.

"And now you have the money to buy an airplane."

"But I have Joey. I have responsibilities. I can't hop in a plane and take off. So why get one? What about you?" He caressed her arm. "What do you want?"

You. A baby. "One of those," she said about the big-screen television to lighten the mood.

Derek stared at the screen and winced. "Bases loaded and he's up to bat. Bad news. He's going to strike out."

"Be an optimist, Derek," Lara teased.

"I'm also a realist. He's struck out the last six times at bat."

"Ye of little faith."

"Want to bet that he'll strike out?"

She slanted a look at him. "Are you being sneaky?"

"Could be." He tucked strands of her hair behind her ear. "You won't know until you accept my bet."

"Hmmm." She gave him a thoughtful stare. "I wonder what the bet could be?"

"I wonder?" he said with a laugh. "Come on. We haven't got all day. He'll be swinging again."

"You're on. If I win, you have to sit through a chick flick with me."

Brows bunching, he sent her a pained look.

"And if you win, what do I owe you?"

He took her wineglass from her hand and set it on the coffee table. "You know."

"That's no bet."

He pulled her down with him and pressed her length against his. "It isn't?"

"No, I'd want to do that, too." As he lightly nibbled at her earlobe, she sighed. "If you win, what do you want?"

"I can't think of anything—" he nuzzled her neck "—that I'd want more than you."

Eyes closing, she giggled when his mouth tickled her. "Is he swinging?"

"Who cares," he murmured, and covered her mouth with his own.

"It was a good movie," Lara insisted when they were leaving the movie theater.

"Not bad." Derek linked his fingers with hers.

"Romantic."

"Every woman in the theater was crying," he said with a hint of disbelief. "What's romantic about that?"

"Okay. The ending was sad," she conceded, and stopped with him beneath a streetlight. "But the rest of the movie was romantic. Like when they took a bubble bath.''

''We've done that,'' he reminded her.

''And it was romantic.''

He looked pleased with himself. ''Every couple in New York takes a carriage ride through Central Park like they did in the movie.''

''Not every couple,'' Lara said.

''Guess I get another point for thinking of that, too.''

His light, airy tone roused her smile. ''Guess you do,'' she agreed. ''Are you getting smug?''

''Definitely.''

''I'm creating a monster by reminding you of all your good qualities, aren't I?''

''Probably.'' He released a low, throaty laugh and drew her into his arms. ''But he's a romantic one.''

Lara leaned back to slip her arms around his neck. ''Yes, he is.'' And he's the man I love. Those words she kept to herself, aware they'd send him running. ''You have a scheduled C-section early in the morning.''

''Are you telling me to go home?''

Certain he had no plan to do that, she delivered a delighted laugh against his lips, then kissed him hard. ''I was thinking we'd better get home quickly.''

Early shifts at the hospital never were easy. Lara yawned several times as she walked down the corridor toward the nurses' station.

"Your mother called," one of the other nurses said.

"Thanks." Lara stopped by a vending machine, and with soda in hand, took her break. While sipping the drink, she punched out her family's number on her cell phone.

"Lara, when are you going to get your test results?" her mother asked after a hello.

Lara cradled the phone between her jaw and her shoulder. "I go tomorrow, Mama."

"Do you want me to go with you?"

"No, I'm fine." She wanted a baby with all her heart, but time spent with Derek forced an obvious realization. "I'm going to be all right, Mama."

"I knew that long ago. What about your handsome doctor? Has he realized yet that he loves you?"

Lara laughed and sank into the closest chair. "Mama, he never said that."

"Words. Who needs words? People put too much importance on romantic words and gifts. How does he act when he's with you? Does he want to be with you? Does he think about your feelings?" She went on quickly before Lara could say anything, "If you were sick would he be here for you?"

Lara knew the answer to that. Derek had shown up at her doctor's waiting room; he'd been there for her.

"How they act. That's what matters."

"Yes," she agreed. But in her heart she knew she needed to hear the words from him.

Derek ended his morning run earlier than usual. Winded, he stilled at the front doorway in response to noise in the kitchen. Since Lara was at the hospital and only one other person had a key to his place, he guessed who was there.

Standing near the sink, Dorothy wiggled fingers in a hello wave at him as he entered the kitchen.

Taking a few minutes to breathe normally, he flopped on a kitchen chair. He smelled the rich aroma of coffee. Frankly his coffee stunk. "Thank you for making that."

"I know how terrible yours usually is," she said as she set a cup before him.

He wiped the back of his hand over his damp face. "Is that why you came this morning?"

"I came because Joey's coming home tomorrow. I needed to make chocolate chip muffins for him. You're going out this evening?" She gestured toward the dry-cleaning bag that Derek had hung on the hallway door yesterday after it was delivered.

"For a moment, I thought you'd taken up mind reading."

"I read the appointment book on your desk. It's a fund-raiser. Are you taking Lara?"

He had no problem with her questions. After years of Dorothy being around, he viewed her nosiness with affection.

"She is—"

He stopped sipping coffee to look at her. He'd thought she'd say fun.

"Different from you," she said instead. "She's so lovely, fun-loving, happy."

He laughed. "What am I? Doom and gloom?"

"You used to be serious most of the time."

"What about when I made a blanket fort with Joey?"

Thoughtfully she stared at him. "Was that BL or SL?" At his frown, she explained, "Before Lara or since Lara."

"Since," he said grudgingly. "But don't I take Joey to the park to play ball?" he asked in his defense.

"You do."

"Dorothy, what's your point?"

"She's good for you."

He said nothing. How could he? She was right. That didn't help him. It made breaking away from Lara harder. She wanted marriage; he didn't. Then there was Joey to consider.

Without his son around, he'd spent every possible moment with Lara. But how could he when Joey was back? He had to think about his son's feelings.

And what about her? She was great for him, but he wasn't for her. The last thing he wanted to do was hurt her when she made him so happy.

Lara finished her early shift at the hospital and wandered toward Manhattan Multiples. The center was buzzing with excitement. One of the women who'd been getting fertility treatments learned she was having sextuplets.

"I can't imagine," Carrie said to Lara when they

were gathering supplies in the supply room. "What would it be like to have that many babies around?"

Lara grabbed a package of swabs. "Hectic." She'd like one, just one. She'd be perfectly satisfied with just one baby.

"Want to have lunch at the grill?"

"Can't. I need to go shopping. Come with me," Lara urged.

"Where are you going?"

"You'll like it."

An hour later Carrie still looked shocked about where Lara had taken her. "I can't believe we're in here. This place is not cheap," she whispered in Lara's ear.

For several seconds since they'd entered the exclusive Manhattan boutique, she and Carrie had been scrutinized by the salesperson, a trim, snooty-looking woman with blond hair slicked back in a chignon.

"Do you feel like Julia Roberts?" Carrie's eyes brightened. "I loved *Pretty Woman,* though I didn't like any of her other movies except *Sleeping With the Enemy.* That was creepy."

Lara eyed a midnight-blue sleeveless dress in silk with a high neckline and a slit that revealed a hint of thigh.

She needed something suitable. Now there was a word from her past. Life held a lot of surprises. She'd always known she had feelings for Derek. A crush on a handsome doctor wasn't so far-fetched for a nurse. But she'd never thought they'd mean anything to each other, never thought he'd hold her, kiss her, make

love with her or care for her. She never thought she'd
want another man who came from the same moneyed
background as James.

"Lara, what do you think of this?"

Lara zeroed in on the red wrap dress Carrie was
gesturing at. "Too evening."

Carrie frowned. "But the party is in the evening."

"The blue would be better." She drew a breath.
"I'd like to try on that one."

The saleswoman offered a tight smile. "Of course.
It's beautiful."

"Yes, it is."

And it's mine, Lara mused, pleased the dress hadn't
been too expensive.

She and Derek paused outside the upscale Manhattan restaurant. French doors opened to the party in
the restaurant's private room. The buzz of conversation filled the room jammed with men in dark suits
and women showing off their best cocktail-hour
finery.

Lara and Derek stopped beneath a crystal chande-
lier as Eloise rushed forward to greet them. "I'm glad
you came." Eloise took Lara's hand and drew back
to peruse her dress. "You look absolutely beautiful,
Lara."

"Thank you. So do you." Eloise was lovely in a
mauve jacket over a matching-colored ankle-length
dress.

"Derek, talk to you-know-who, will you?" Eloise
said in a whisper.

As she stepped away, Lara swung a questioning look up at him. She'd pulled her hair back. With the movement of her head, several strands brushed her neck. "You-know-who?"

He fingered one of the pearls dangling from her ear. "The tall, distinguished-looking man in the corner sandwiched between two women. You do look gorgeous, you know."

"Thank you. But who is he?"

"He's a fertility specialist from California, who we're interested in bringing to Manhattan Multiples."

"You'd better talk to him, then."

His touch on the back of her neck was featherlight. "I'll only be gone for a moment."

Lara gave him a reassuring smile and scanned the room. Arms outstretched, people grazed cheeks, greeted each other with obligatory social greetings.

Lara skirted around two couples debating the merits of the new school superintendent. Politics dominated the conversations. She heard a sprinkling of talk about trips.

"I spent last holiday in St. Moritz," one woman said. "We leave next Friday for our vacation home in Barcelona," her companion replied.

The moneyed crowd was what the center needed. Though from a different background, Lara had felt no discomfort around them. Everyone she'd met had been friendly. In fact, most of them had been interested in learning about the woman Derek Cross was with. That was fine. But the lack of laughter bothered her. She was used to noisy. If more than four of her family gathered, voices rose several octaves in conversation, and there was always laughter.

"Lara? It is Lara, isn't it?" a woman said, approaching from her right.

Lara stilled and faced her and her companion. In their midsixties, they pried, asking at least a dozen questions. Lara maneuvered conversation away from her and Derek and toward Manhattan Multiples, impressing on them how important the center was.

As they nodded in agreement, she made eye contact with Derek. From across the room, he picked up on her plea for rescuing. The moment he sidled up to her, she linked her hand with his.

"Hello, ladies." He flashed his best smile at them. They nearly giggled like schoolgirls. "Are you hungry, Lara?"

"Starving." She eyed the group gathered at the buffet table. "So is everyone, it seems." She waited until they'd taken several steps from the women, and were weaving their way around people to reach the buffet table. "Thank you for rescuing me. Did you influence the doctor?"

"He's willing to come and see Eloise." He stopped with her and picked up a plate. "What's this?" he asked a white-jacketed server, referring to one of the dishes.

"Salmon in a merlot sauce, sir."

"I'll have that."

Lara chose a chicken dish. "What time does Joey come home tomorrow?"

"In the morning."

Would tonight be the end? Lara vowed to have no regrets. He had been fair and honest with her from day one. No, he hadn't or he wouldn't have made it so easy for her to fall in love with him.

"Derek? Derek, that is you, isn't it?" a deep male voice asked from the other side of the table.

Derek turned without a frown, seeming to recognize the voice. "Good evening, Senator Trumbell."

"Lloyd," he reminded him.

Touching Lara's elbow, he urged her to move forward and stand beside him.

With his introduction, the senator grinned. "It's a pleasure, Ms. Mancini."

Lara returned his smile. "For me, also."

"I'd say Eloise is having a very successful fundraiser."

"She has another planned, a bigger one," Lara reminded him. "We hope you'll attend."

"I'll certainly try. You volunteer your services at her center, don't you, Derek?" To Derek's nod, he smiled. "Very commendable." He looked behind them, appeared distracted but didn't move away. "I heard Emerson is back in the States. Has your father been back very long?"

Derek offered what Lara viewed as a strained smile. "A few days."

"Tell him I said hello. That he should call me."

"I will, Senator."

The man smiled as he pivoted toward a group gathered around Eloise.

"Do you hobnob with the president, too?" Lara teased.

His hand shifted to the sharp angle of her hip. "My father does."

"Really?"

"Ambassadors, foreign diplomats. He knows them all."

"An important man?"

He maintained a dispassionate look. "He thinks so."

A tinge of sadness rippled through her but had no chance to grab hold.

"Hello, Derek," another male voice intruded from behind them.

Every muscle in Lara's body tensed. She didn't need to turn around to know who stood behind them. She'd heard that same voice whispering sweet nothings in her ear for months. Straightening her back, she turned away from the buffet table to face the blond-haired man.

A faint frown furrowed Derek's brow. "James. I believe you know each other," Derek said, placing a hand on the small of her back in a reassuring gesture.

Apparently James had spotted Derek but not her before he'd come over. She felt overwhelming satisfaction at the dumbstruck expression on his face.

He recovered quickly. Faint lines crinkled at the corners of pale blue eyes. "Lara, it's been years."

"Yes, it has." She'd thought she loved him, wanted to marry him and now couldn't think of a word to say to him.

"Well—" He waited for her to start conversation. That was natural. She'd always had the gift of the gab, but she had no intention of making the moment easier on him.

"My wife is there." He pointed in the direction of a brunette in her second trimester of pregnancy.

She was one of his own, Lara assumed. His wife wore an ivory-colored, one-shouldered dress with an empire waistline. Lara had seen a similar designer dress in a magazine one of her pregnant cousins had bought. "Congratulations, James."

Dumbly he stared at her.

"You are going to be a father, aren't you?"

"Oh." Realization slipped over his face. "Yes. Yes, I am."

"Congratulations," she said again.

He offered a quick nod of his head. "Thank you. And are you—" He paused, looked at Derek.

Lara jumped in. "We work at Manhattan Multiples."

"You do? Oh, that explains why you're here."

Of course he'd need some reason. Lara was about to excuse herself. Fortunately he did it first. "Good to see you—both," he said, looking from her to Derek.

"He seems to have gotten his wish," she said when he went to his wife.

As if trying to decipher what wasn't visible, Derek narrowed his eyes at her. "What's that?"

"An heir."

Puzzlement bunched his brows. If he had a question, he didn't ask it. "Do you want to eat outside?"

She traced his gaze to French doors that led out to a courtyard. "Yes." The room suddenly felt stuffy and uncomfortable. Too many people, too many different fragrances, too much conversation. All she wanted was to be alone with him, hold him, let him know how important he was to her.

With plates in hands, they wandered through French doors onto a brick-paved terrace. Small, sparkling, white lights were strung on the trees and along a trellis. A night sky with a full moon added to the romantic mood.

"What did you mean when you said he'd gotten his wish?" She wasn't surprised he didn't wait to find out what was bothering him. "You wanted children then, too, didn't you?"

"Yes." She met his quizzical stare. "But I wasn't suitable."

"Suitable?" He angled a frown her way. "For what? To be his wife?"

"He and his mother informed me that I wasn't."

"You said that before, mentioned your family—"

"There's nothing wrong with my family." She wanted him to know the truth. "That was about me. My questionable fertility."

"What?" He set his plate aside on a small, round patio table.

"The fertility factor," Lara said, facing him. "It was important. James needed an heir. Even back then I couldn't be sure I'd be able to have babies."

"That's why he—"

"Dumped me." She lifted her chin a notch, met his gaze. "I might not provide a Braden heir, they said. I, too, was a lousy marriage risk, Derek."

"Lara." His voice softened. "He really was a fool." Taking her hand, he pressed his lips to her knuckles. "Don't let him hurt you anymore."

"I'm not," she assured him. Tenderly she placed fingers on his smooth jaw. Even before she'd begun seeing him, she'd stopped caring about James, about the hurt he'd caused her with his cruel words.

As Derek drew her into his arms, she slipped her hand onto his shoulder. Music, light and distant, drifted to them from the restaurant's piano bar. "Dancing with you has become a favorite pastime of mine."

Her eyes fluttered and closed. She needed this, wanted to be in his embrace. With her temple against his cheek, they swayed to the music, barely moving. "Me, too," she murmured.

When they'd danced at her cousin's wedding, she'd never expected he'd be spending every possible hour with her. During the past week while Joey had been gone, they'd sat in a bubble bath surrounded by candles and had sipped champagne, then had made love. They'd sung a duet while he'd pounded out "Heart and Soul" on the piano. She'd sipped wine while listening to him play Mozart. She'd even run in the park with him. They'd slept together, and awakened to the sight of each other.

Everything between them was becoming more intense. And despite all that, he expected her to believe they wouldn't be together, that nothing was forever between them.

He'd asked what was on her wish list. He was. He'd always been since the day she'd met him. Yet, she'd never really believed they were meant for each other.

That had been James's fault. He'd weakened her, made her doubt herself. But never had the issue of suitability existed between Derek and her. Never had it mattered how different their backgrounds were. He'd fit in with her family as well as she'd blended into his social life. If only he wanted all that she did. If only he wanted her forever.

Chapter Thirteen

Lara eyed the digital clock beside her bed. Derek had gone home, wanting to be there when Joey arrived. Sleeping alone had felt strange after so many nights together. She considered staying in bed a moment longer, had started to close her eyes when the phone rang.

"Hi, Lara. It's Joey," the voice said.

No phone call could have surprised her more. "Joey, did you dial my number by yourself?"

"You don't dial, Lara. You push buttons."

She smiled. "That's right. So did you push the buttons?"

"Uh-huh. But Mommy found your phone number."

So Rose was near.

"Lara, when am I going to see you?"

"That's right. I'm supposed to read a story."

"Uh-huh. That's what I told Mommy. We're going to the park. Want to go?"

"Let me talk to your mommy."

"Mommy said please."

"I did," Rose said lightly, taking over the phone. "Meet us, Lara."

"I'd love to."

Within the hour she was dressed and sitting on a park bench beside Rose. "Joey is talking nonstop about getting a puppy," Lara said to her as Joey went off to play with a few other children.

Rose smiled, shrugging a shoulder. "His father holds the answer to that."

Lara hadn't noticed any sadness in Joey's eyes. "Did you tell Joey you'd be leaving?"

"Yes. And emotionally I seesaw between wanting to go and staying here. Leaving Joey makes my heart ache. To some people I probably seem like an awful mother."

Lara touched her hand. "I doubt that. You wouldn't go if you weren't convinced you needed to."

A sadness remained in Rose's eyes, but she nodded. "The research they're doing could be invaluable to many children one day. I believe the research department is close to a breakthrough. Children. They're all that ever mattered to me."

"Me, too," Lara admitted.

Rose gave her a quick smile. "You need some of your own."

Lara capsulized her medical problem.

"Surely you know not to give up hope."

"Ask anyone who knows me," Lara said with a lightness that was forced.

"I'm glad you're around for Joey."

Barely Lara maintained a smile. Didn't Rose realize Derek wouldn't allow anyone to get too close to their son?

"Joey is really fond of you."

"If you don't mind me saying so, I love him."

Rose's smile widened. "When I said fond, that was an understatement. Joey loves you, too."

Lara doubted few other words could fill her with so much joy.

Rose touched her hand. "I'm glad you do. Children need as much love as they can get." A weariness suddenly entered her voice. "This is so difficult. I assured Joey I'd call him a lot and be home as much as I could. I know that Derek will make it easier on him. I'm always amazed at what a great job Derek's done with him, especially since Derek always expects people to let him down."

"Because of his parents?"

"So he's talked about them to you." She glanced Joey's way for a moment. "There are few people Derek would share childhood memories with."

"I've been told that I'm pushy."

"I'm sure that it has more to do with his feelings for you. Derek is never pushed into anything. He's such a fine person despite a childhood with unfeeling parents.''

People he could never trust to keep promises, Lara mused. ''It's difficult for me to understand people treating a child, especially their own, like that.'' Lara hesitated to go on. What she was about to say bordered on private information between him and Rose.

Rose inclined her head questioningly. ''Lara—what aren't you saying?''

''He told me that you and he married for the sake of your careers.''

''Actually I pushed for marriage, felt it would look better for me as a pediatrician. But he never wanted marriage. I convinced him that a married obstetrician would be viewed more favorably. Oh, don't misunderstand. We thought we loved each other. But we learned we were not *the* love in each other's lives. And from the beginning of our relationship, he told me that he didn't believe in promises.''

''He told me that, too,'' Lara admitted.

Rose gave a shake of her head. ''I'd hoped—well, trust is difficult to give, isn't it?''

Without more being said, Lara understood Derek had never learned to trust. Oh, he might accept someone's words that they'd do something or be somewhere, but he protected his heart, never trusted anyone with it—except Joey.

Before saying goodbye to Rose and Joey, she assured him that she'd be over to read the story. She left but didn't hurry. She talked a good game about never giving up, but hope was elusive sometimes.

In a few minutes, she'd be in the doctor's office, and she was clinging to the hope that she hadn't lost all chance to conceive. Look at Gena, she reminded herself as she entered the doctor's waiting room. Gena had thought she'd never have a child, and now she was pregnant.

After taking a seat, Lara pulled out her knitting. With luck, she'd finish the afghan before her cousin's baby was born. Repeatedly she glanced at her wristwatch. She was no different from anyone else. She hated a doctor's waiting room.

Nervous about the results of her tests, she dropped a stitch for the second time in the past five minutes. If she kept knitting, she'd probably make a mess and end up starting over.

Placing the needles and yarn in her oversize shoulder bag, she glanced at her wristwatch again. Why did time tick away so slowly during difficult moments, and speed by when all was right with the world?

"Ms. Mancini," a nurse at an open door said.

Lara stood, and walked toward her.

The nurse smiled.

She smiled back, but she felt like the condemned man on death row, taking his last few steps before all his dreams ended.

"She said she'd come over tonight, Daddy," Joey said excitedly over the phone, after telling him that he and Rose had seen Lara at the park.

"She did?" Why had Rose met her is what Derek

wanted to know. Was his ex looking for someone to fill the void for Joey when she went to Europe? "We'll talk tonight, Joey."

Finished with hospital rounds, he strode toward the exit. Though Lara hadn't said anything about her appointment, he'd remembered that she was supposed to get test results today. He wanted to be with her. He didn't allow himself to consider how her news would affect them. He only knew he wanted her smiling again.

"Dr. Cross. ICU—stat."

Frowning, Derek stopped steps from the exit and whipped around.

Nearly two hours passed before he was free. Worried about Lara, he called her cell phone and her home phone number, and got no answer. Dammit, what if the news had been bad? Was she off somewhere crying? He couldn't contact her family, alarm them.

At a loss where to call, he took a chance and headed across the street to Manhattan Multiples. A quick question to Josie sent him rushing upstairs. He'd seen the woman's smile before he'd dashed away. It didn't matter to him if others learned he was asking for Lara. He just wanted to see her, make sure she was all right.

The moment he entered the staff lounge and saw her, relief rushed through him. Her profile to him, she looked with unseeing eyes down at her hands wrapped around a white coffee cup. "Lara."

It seemed to take forever before her eyes met his.

"You went to the doctor." Stepping near, he removed the cup from her hand. Whatever her answer was, he wanted to be holding her when she told him. "What were the results of the tests?"

"It's—" She paused as if stunned by her own thought. "It's good news." Her eyes fixed on him and brightened. "It's not endometriosis. An infection." She tossed back her head, her smile filled with happiness, then collapsed against him. "It can be cured, Derek."

Gently he ran a soothing hand over her hair. All day he'd been waiting to feel her in his arms, he realized.

She pulled back, looked up at him, her eyes bright with tears of joy. "I'm so happy. Everything is fine." She released another delighted laugh. "No, it's wonderful. With treatment, antibiotics, the doctor said I should have no trouble getting pregnant."

"That's wonderful." He meant those words. He'd wanted this for her. Now she could have the family she longed for, could hold her own baby some day. But he wasn't the one to offer that future. There was the thought he'd dodged for hours. "Have you called your family?"

"Not yet."

Do it now, he berated himself. "I'll tell Joey that you'll be busy tonight."

She went still. "Busy?"

He battled himself to let her go because he wanted

to keep holding her. "I heard you saw him and Rose today."

"They called. They asked me to meet them." She fixed a puzzled look on him.

That was his fault. With too many emotions teetering close to the surface, he was having a difficult time easing into this moment. Possibly there was no easy way to end everything with her. "Your family will expect you."

"I'm sure they will." In a small show of nerves, she brushed back tendrils of hair. "Something else is going on here, isn't it? You're not pleased that I met Joey and Rose, are you?"

He heard the forced calmness in her voice, knew he was making her feel bad. "All of a sudden lots of people want into our lives. What will Joey feel when they don't anymore?"

"Lots of people?" Confusion dulled her eyes. "Are we talking about me or—"

He damned himself for taking her smile away.

"Or your father?" A need to understand flickered in her eyes. "Couldn't this work out well?"

"He is who he is." Derek wasn't sure what would happen with his father, but he knew that he wouldn't let him hurt Joey.

But he might.

Right now would be the best time to finish this— before Rose left, before Joey leaned more on Lara. And then there was Lara to think about. She had a chance to have what she really wanted. "Lara, I'll never be the man you need."

He saw her draw a deep breath, a calming one. "You say that, but—"

He wouldn't let her talk. He needed to have his say before he did something foolish and changed his mind. "You made the mistake of believing in us. I never have. I never expected anything from you."

"I love you. Love can't be switched on and off."

He knew she believed that, but hearing the words rocked him. "Don't," he said. Love. He didn't want to talk about love. "I've already learned I can't make marriage work. You need to find the person who'll give you what you want. That's not me."

"Wrong! You won't give it a chance. Why are you trying so hard to convince me? Or is it yourself...?" She stopped in response to his name being called over the center's paging system.

He said the obvious. "I have to go."

Lips tight, she said nothing, just shook her head at him.

He swung around. Heading toward the nurses' station, he resisted an urge to look back at her. He'd done the right thing. Oh, hell, had he? Why couldn't he get her hurt look out of his mind? He had done right by her. He'd have hurt her more eventually. In time, she'd realize that.

Under his breath, he cursed. Already he missed her. How had his life gotten so complicated suddenly? Keeping it simple had been his goal for years.

When had he dropped his guard?

Fool. That's what he really was. Keeping everything simple had ended the first time he kissed her.

* * *

On edge, he battled his foul mood to prevent Joey from seeing it. That evening's dinner was Joey's favorite, chicken strips. Though Derek didn't mind them occasionally, Joey favored the crunchy, greasy strips at least twice a week.

"We should have waited for Lara." Eyes downward, he pouted at the last bite of chicken. "She'd like this dinner."

"Joey, she's been busy."

"She promised she'd be by tonight."

He'd heard his share of empty promises. In fairness to Lara, after what he'd done earlier, he doubted she'd even remember that offhand promise to his son. On a professional level, he expected her to request a different doctor to work with at the center. He expected nothing to be simple or easy between them from this point on.

"But she promised, Daddy."

Don't count on anyone. Derek remembered his own heartache, knew how much it hurt to wait for someone who never came. One Christmas Day when he'd sat beneath the tree with the nanny and the butler nearby, he hadn't cared what was in the presents. He'd wanted his parents. But they'd never come. "Come on. It's bath time."

"What if something happened to her?"

His son worried with the best of them. "Nothing happened to her." Except your father acted like a jerk with her. "After your bath, I'll read the story to you tonight."

"If Lara's late, you mean."

Derek gave up trying to prepare him for her not showing up.

No longer seeming concerned, Joey rattled on about his best friend's hamsters.

"No hamsters, Joey."

Bath time was one of Joey's favorite times of the day. He usually filled half the tub with toys, boats, rubber alligators, a shark that dived under water, even his fishing pole and magnetized fish.

Sitting in the tub, he aimed the shark, sent it into a nosedive under the water. It emerged at the other end of the tub. "I don't want a hamster. I want to talk about a dog. We could call a boy dog Sam and a girl dog Molly, Daddy." He paused in pushing a toy boat through the water. "Do you think we could get a dog?"

Derek sat on a stool near him and gestured at Joey's arm. "Wash your elbows, too." As a kid, he'd wanted a dog. "You won't be home enough," his mother had pointed out. She was right. He'd spent more time in boarding school than at the house.

A dog. He stared at his son. Head bent, making putt-putt noises, Joey pushed the boat again. Dorothy was a good sport and would do anything for Joey. She'd make sure a dog would have food and water. She'd help housebreak it. And on weekends or his days off, he and Joey could walk it and play with it in the park. The other days were no problem, either. He'd hire a professional dog walker for those days when he couldn't do that job. "Joey—" He waited for him to look up. "I think we'll take a ride to Grandpa Joe's when those puppies are ready for a home."

His eyes went wide, and on a squeal of joy, he threw himself at Derek. His son's wet, soapy arms slapped at his neck. "We're really getting a puppy?"

"Yes, we are," Derek answered. "Yes, we are." As he grabbed a towel and wrapped it around him, Joey smacked a wet kiss on his cheek. Derek held him close. Nothing smelled sweeter than a child after a bath.

"Wait until I tell Lara."

Mentally he swore as much at himself as the situation as he caught himself wishing she would come. No, it was best that she didn't. Perhaps Joey wouldn't miss her too much. Of course he would. It was a double whammy with Rose and Lara missing from his life at the same time. Derek knew nothing he did would help his son. He was going to be hurt. "Joey—"

"Daddy, the doorbell went buzz."

"Pj's are on the bed." He ruffled his son's short hair, then let him go. "Hop into them."

When he scooted off, Derek went toward the door. In no mood for company, he took his time opening it. The moment he did, emotion flooded him with longing.

"Before you say anything, I'm here for Joey," Lara announced.

He ached, wanted to take her in his arms. His heart lurched with misgivings about what he'd said to her earlier. Had he made a mistake? Just seeing her made the empty hours without her disappear.

"Where is he?" she asked, and breezed past him into the foyer.

Don't touch. He was being a fool again. Only a fool believed in love, in marriage. Don't even think about touching her. "In the bedroom."

"Lara, Lara!" Joey said excitedly from his bedroom doorway and darted down the hall to leap into her arms.

Holding him tightly, she laughed. "Hello, yourself. I'm here to read that story."

"It's a good story, Lara," he said when she was heading toward the bedroom with him in her arms. "It's all about—"

As they disappeared into Joey's room, Derek wandered into the kitchen. He felt like hell. He grabbed a medical journal from the counter, read an article, but couldn't concentrate and tossed it onto the table. All he could think about was the two of them. As if a movie was flashing before him, he remembered every time he'd seen them laughing with their heads close or holding hands or hugging.

He really hadn't expected her to show up, but he had thought she'd call, he realized at that moment. Responsible, reliable, she cared too much about others' feelings not to call Joey, to let him know that she wasn't coming.

So she was near. Near enough for him to tell her he'd made a mistake. At the sound of footsteps behind him, he swung around. She was near enough for him to touch, to hold, to kiss.

She stood in the soft light of the hallway. "I'd wondered where you were."

"Thanks for remembering your promise to Joey. I didn't expect you to come."

"Oh, I know you didn't."

The edge to her voice alerted him. He'd never doubted that she'd tell him off at some moment. She felt deeply in joy and sorrow.

"You expect nothing from anyone. Well, I'm good for my promises. I told you that before."

He might have smiled at her spirited manner if he hadn't seen such hurt in her eyes.

"It occurred to me I don't like being dumped."

"Lara—"

"At least, not without having my say. I knew you'd end this. I tried to prepare for it, but I couldn't." For a second she sounded more angry at herself than him. "You push love away, but then that's easier than trusting or taking a chance and loving someone." No anger now, just bafflement in her voice. "But I've never given you a reason not to trust me."

"This has nothing to do with you. It's me." He let out a breath. "I'm like them. I've proven that I'm a lousy risk for marriage just like they were."

"You believe that you're like your parents?" In what he thought might be an effort to stifle emotion, she raised her chin as if she was daring someone to take a poke at it. "You're nothing like them," she challenged. "You told me you were never able to depend on them."

He heard an appeal in her voice for him to believe what she was saying.

"Yet, you've never let your son down."

"Lara, this is getting us nowhere."

"You're not like them. Because of you, Joey feels loved. I've never seen a more loving father than you are with him." She shoved up the strap of her shoulder bag. "Just look in your son's eyes, and you'll know. You'll never be like them."

As she reached out for him, he pulled back. "You should go," he said, steeling himself.

Pain clouded her eyes. "You always said I'd get hurt. I guess you were right."

He watched her turn away, nearly called out to her. She had no idea how much he'd wanted to believe her, believe in them.

And do what?

Hurt her more? Destroy her dreams?

No, this was best for her. He'd done the right thing. Deliberately he'd angered her to make her back away. She deserved what she wanted, and she wouldn't find that with him.

He drew a hard breath and strode toward his son's bedroom. He should feel satisfaction, relief. Instead, he felt a pain in the middle of his chest. How could he ever forget the way she'd looked at him before she'd left?

"Daddy?" Joey called from the bedroom.

"Coming." Being noble stunk, he decided.

Sitting up in his bed, Joey held his favorite book. "I really like this story. Lara reads good."

Derek settled on the bed beside him. "How many times did you have her read it to you?" He knew his son would listen to it over and over again.

"Only once. She'll read it when she comes again."

She's not coming again. He held back those words. "Come on. Hop on. I'll give you a piggyback ride to the bathroom. It's teeth-brushing time."

"I knew she'd come," Joey said in his ear. "I told you, didn't I?"

"Yeah, you did," Derek said, and set Joey's feet down on the stool in front of the sink.

"Daddy, I told Lara we're going to get a puppy. She could go with us when we do, couldn't she?"

Derek avoided answering. "How did you know she'd come tonight?"

"'Cause she promised."

"Joey, people don't always keep promises."

"You do."

Touched that he trusted him without doubt, Derek ran a hand over his son's head. "Yes."

"And Mommy does. And Lara does. Because she loves me. Like you do. She said so."

How simple he made that sound.

Head bent, his son squeezed at the toothpaste tube with his small fingers. "I can't get any out of it."

"Let me." Derek squeezed the tube until the aqua-colored, bubblegum-flavored gel oozed out. "Here you go."

In the mirror, he stared at his son. *Look in your son's eyes,* Lara had said.

"I'm all done." Joey flashed small, white teeth at him.

Love. He saw it. Maybe Joey understood love better than he did. If you love someone, you had to believe in and trust that person not to hurt you. Lara had said she loved him. But he hadn't believed or trusted her.

"Tomorrow, can Dorothy take me to have lunch with you?"

"Sure she can."

"Do you want a hug?"

Derek yanked himself from thoughts, looked down at him. "What?"

"You're looking funny at me. Do you want a hug?"

My son. "Yes." Derek smiled. "Yes, I do."

Stretching up, Joey coiled small, slender arms around his neck and squeezed gently but firmly.

Lightly Derek smoothed a hand over the back of Joey's head, held him near. It took effort not to hug too hard. Never would his son have doubts about his love for him.

Drawing back, Joey kept his face within inches of Derek's eyes. "I love you, Daddy."

As a tightness clutched at his throat, he pulled in a deep breath, hugged his son tighter. *Love.* There had been a time when he'd believed no one loved him. "I know, Joey. I love you, too."

Chapter Fourteen

Sleep didn't help. Lara awoke in the morning with an expected headache. After taking a few aspirins, she worked hard to fight the sadness heavy in her chest. She needed to see her mother. Her family would expect more than a phone call about her test results. It wouldn't be easy to veil true feelings in front of them. Her mother would expect smiles, joy. Lara struggled to work up that mood while she drove to her parents' home.

"That's wonderful news from the doctor," her father said after Lara announced the results of her tests. Family had gathered around. She hadn't expected to see two of her brothers and her one sister there. Perhaps this was best. They'd spread the news to the rest, saving her from having to make numerous phone calls.

When they wandered into the kitchen with their father for his specialty, blueberry pancakes, Lara found herself alone with her mother. "I can't stay. I have to get to the center. I'm due there this morning."

"I'm so pleased for you, darling."

Lara forced a smile, but tears smarted her eyes. She fought them, blinked hard. She couldn't remember any man making her cry. Even when she'd broken up with James, she hadn't wept.

"Those aren't tears of joy," her mother said. "Tell me." There was no point trying to avoid the "motherly stare" as Lara's brothers and sisters called her I-can-see-inside-you look. "Tell me what happened with him. Why are you unhappy? He loves you, too."

"Does he?"

"That was clear at the wedding."

"You could tell?"

Her mother took her hands. "Everyone could."

"Mama," Angela yelled from the doorway. "Where is your cinnamon?"

Her mother waved her off. "In the cupboard above the stove. Go away," she said, never taking her eyes off Lara. "Why doesn't he realize that?"

From the kitchen, Lara heard her brothers Nick and Mario arguing about a baseball game.

"You're both wrong," Angie yelled.

Male laughter answered her.

Lara had thought she'd never feel like smiling again, but just being around them made her feel better. How lucky she was, she realized as she thought of all the love and laughter her family had shared.

Her heart ached for Derek whenever she thought about his childhood.

"Lara, why doesn't he?"

How could she explain? He expected to fail at emotional involvement because his parents had. Lara believed he was far too intelligent to believe something like that was inherited like blue eyes or dark hair. This was about a man who'd never gotten over a child's pain. "Because he pushes everyone away before they get too close." Because he'd never had what had always been part of her life—love.

The last place Derek wanted to be was at the Manhattan Hotel, but he had no choice except to keep the meeting with his father. He doubted the visit would be long. They had nothing in common and little to talk about.

He entered the hotel and headed toward its five-star restaurant. Even from a distance he thought his father looked tired. Perhaps from working too hard. Workaholics rarely slowed down willingly.

"Derek." He stood, folded his *Wall Street Journal.*

"Sir. Sit," Derek urged.

The years were being kind to him. His skin remained taut, only a few deep lines crinkled from the corners of his eyes. A beefy man with gray hair cropped short, Emerson Wentworth Cross was an inch shorter than Derek's six foot four. He was an intimidating man. In his custom-tailored suit, he stood before Derek as solemn-looking as ever. "You look different."

I'm happier, Derek wanted to say. That's what was different about him. He'd learned there was a place in his heart that still wanted to draw love in. How could he explain to this man, to this stranger, that his own child had taught him he wasn't meant to be alone?

"I ordered a drink," he said when they were seated.

Around them people chatted in hushed, dignified tones, silverware softly clicked. "I'll have coffee," Derek told the waitress.

"Are you going back to work?"

"I never know."

"You should have chosen a different field of medicine."

He kept a defensive edge out of his voice. "I like this one." His father had remarked before that he'd made a poor choice. Obstetrics offered no prestige or recognition. "I help bring new life into the world," Derek said simply. "How is international finance?"

"I'm doing well. Working less." He paused. "You look surprised."

"I am." He never thought his father would take time to relax.

"How is your son? He's how old?"

Derek looked up as the server placed coffee before him. "He's five."

"Good boy?"

For a split second Derek considered whipping out his wallet to show him Joey's photo, but didn't. "Wonderful."

"Smart?"

"And funny."

His father was quiet for a moment. "Polite?"

"Yes, but mischievous."

"He's like you, then?"

Thoughtfully Derek stared at him.

"You made me laugh," he said as an explanation.

When? He'd never heard his father laugh.

"Remember when you used to jump for the basketball rim to show me how much you'd grown?"

Needing time, Derek sipped his coffee while he absorbed what his father had just said. Had he really watched him?

"Or remember when you brought that motorcycle home?" He chuckled. "Your mother had fits. She was certain you'd be a hoodlum. You were so pleased with yourself. So proud of that motorcycle."

No, he'd been smug, not proud. He'd bought the motorcycle with his own money, hadn't wanted it— not really. He'd bought it to get a reaction out of them. His mother had ranted and raved. Maybe he'd done it because it was rare to have them both at the house, even for a day.

She'd been going to join friends on the French Riviera that evening, and his father was heading for London. He'd wanted them to pay attention. Only his mother had, he'd thought. He'd believed his father had been closeted in his office, on the phone, fielding calls from his international office. Derek had thought he hadn't even watched him. But he'd seen. He'd stood by a window on the second floor and had watched him.

"I was amazed—proud."

Proud? "Why?" Derek asked warily.

"You were so young. Thirteen. You couldn't ride it on the street, but you bought it anyway. I'd never had that kind of gumption. I did what I was told. You were always your own person." He looked uncomfortable with his own weakness. "Is your son like you?"

"A little." Proud. He'd been proud of him. Mentally Derek swore that he was making too much of simple praise from this man.

"You don't need my money, do you? You're an important doctor."

More praise. Derek damned a desire to cling to every favorable word. "No, I don't."

His father cleared his throat. "Does your boy know he has another grandfather?"

"Rose insisted on putting your photo up in his room."

"She did?" He smiled. "That was kind of her. You know, I hardly knew her."

How could he know her? He'd only met her once. At his mother's funeral. "She wanted Joey to know what you looked like."

"Is she still in your life?"

"We're friends."

"Your mother and I didn't do so well after the divorce. Is there anyone else in your life?"

Derek was slow to answer. Had he ever had such

a lengthy conversation with him before? "There's a nurse." What was happening with Lara was private.

"Would you let me see Joseph?" he asked with what sounded like uncertainty in his voice.

Why now? "What happened in your life? You said you're not sick."

"No, I'm not." His gray head bent. "Someone I knew died," he said, staring into his drink. "His last words were for me to tell his son he loved him. But I didn't know anything about this man. I'd known him twenty years and knew his son's name, but not where to find him. And I thought about what if it had been me dying. I wouldn't want to have to tell someone else to relay those words to my son." He fixed a look on Derek, one that used to root him to a spot. "I know you wouldn't believe me if I said them now, but maybe—maybe someday. I'm aware that I haven't always been the best father, but I'll—"

Derek cut him off. "Don't make promises."

For the first time in his life, Derek saw emotion in his father's eyes—sadness. Sadness he'd caused. "I won't." Lowering his head, he checked his watch.

Derek had expected him to do that before this. "An appointment?"

"I suppose I should leave." When Derek didn't respond, his father heaved a sigh.

Derek met his frown with his own. He'd die inside if Joey did this to him. He knew his rejection wouldn't hurt his father the same way, but he had to be fair to him.

"Is it too late?"

Repeatedly he'd given his heart to this man. "No," he said quickly before he let logic instead of emotion control the outcome. "No, it's not too late."

"I'd like to see you—and the boy. Get to know both of you. Do you feel that would be possible?"

Derek drew a hard breath against the pressure in his chest. "Joey just returned to town. I'll call you," he said to avoid a definite answer.

"Anytime." His father offered a halfhearted smile. "Whatever is best for you."

He doesn't believe me, Derek knew. Did he remember all the times he'd said something similar and hadn't meant the words? I'm not you, Derek wanted to say.

"You let me know."

Family is important. Think about today. Tomorrow. Not the past, Lara had insisted. "How about Friday night? Seven," Derek said before he reconsidered. "Is that good for you?"

"It's perfect." A smile sprang to his father's face. "I'll be there."

"Okay." Derek let out a breath to steady his voice. "See you."

"Son—"

With his back to him, Derek closed his eyes for a second. *Son.* A hell of a long time had passed since he'd yearned to hear him say that. "What?" he asked, facing him.

His father's damp eyes met his. "Thank you."

Deep down, some of the boy still remained in the man he was, still yearned for all he hadn't had. "Let's take it one step at a time. Okay?'' Nothing had changed. He still wanted to believe him, he realized. ''I'll see you Friday.''

Exiting the hotel, he didn't need to think about what had happened. He knew. After all these years, he'd learned that he had been right. He really was just like his father. He'd been afraid. Like him, Derek realized.

Afraid to love.

Understanding Derek's decision didn't make accepting it any easier for Lara. She was suddenly in a no-win situation. After learning about all that Derek had gone through as a child and how it had affected him, she'd made a decision about herself.

She wanted any child she had to know the love of both parents. She wanted her child to have parents who not only loved him or her but also each other. Since Derek was that man and denied wanting everything she longed for, she'd never have a child of her own, she knew now.

Her heart ached with the thought, with all she'd lost. She'd met a man she loved. She was able to have the child she longed for. If only he'd let them.

Entering Manhattan Multiples later that morning, Lara faced another problem. She had no intention of leaving the center. She believed in it too much to give up her volunteer work, but it might be best if she worked with another doctor.

Aware Derek was scheduled to arrive around noon, she thought it best if she was out to lunch when he came. On her break, she wandered down to the reception area to ask Josie what time she was taking lunch.

Talking on the phone, Josie raised a hand in a gesture to wait a moment. Nearby, Eloise stood in the doorway of the center's meeting room. Lara couldn't recall a scheduled staff meeting. As Josie ended her phone conversation, Lara leaned over and whispered, "Was there a special meeting today?"

"Oh, no. But I think a new fertility specialist is going to move here from California and volunteer his services."

So Derek had convinced the man to join them. "That's good. When are you going out for lunch?"

"I have to—" Josie went silent, her eyes widening at something behind Lara. "Oh, my."

Conversation in the room stopped. Heads swung toward the entrance. Slowly Lara turned.

At the double glass doors, a beaming Joey stood beside Derek. Lara thought she was seeing things. The cool Dr. Derek Cross was carrying a bunch of bobbing balloons. One red balloon bobbing in the air above Joey's head bore a message: "Will you marry us?"

Josie was wide-eyed. "Lara, is that for you?"

Marry us. Consciously she had to draw a breath. Not taking her eyes off him and Joey, she moved forward.

"Hi, Lara." Joey held out the balloon string. "This is for you." A giggle rode on his voice. "It says—"

Derek touched his son's shoulder. "Joey, I need to

say some things to Lara.'' Angling a glance toward
the far end of the reception room, he nodded at Eloise.
''Go with Mrs. Vale for a few minutes.''

''Daddy—''

A smile flittered at his lips as he gave his son a
reassuring squeeze on the shoulder. ''I'll do my
best.''

Lara found herself smiling. It was the first time in
hours. ''Nice balloon.''

''I thought—'' He looked away to see Joey standing beside Eloise.

Lara had heard a noticeable roughness in his voice.
''You thought—''

''I've been an idiot. I'm sorry.'' With a look to the
side, he frowned, seeming to notice then that they
weren't alone. ''I could do this somewhere more private, but I don't want to wait to say this. I'm sorry,''
he said, speaking low to keep their conversation between them.

She wanted to wrap her arms around him, but because they were surrounded by others, she merely
touched his wrist. ''You said that.''

''No, I'm sorry about everything I said, about how
dumb I've acted.'' His eyes had a sadness in them
that she'd never seen before. ''I turned my back on
you, pushed you away, not because I didn't love you,
but because I did, because—''

Briefly, she looked away to stifle tears. ''Derek—''

''No, wait. You deserve more. I'm not great at beg-
ging, but—''

She pressed her fingertips to his lips.

Gently he caught her hand. "You were right," he went on. "I made myself believe that I was like my parents."

"You know you're not, don't you?"

"But I am. They were afraid to love, to open their hearts to anyone, not even each other." He took a step closer, lightly touched her waist. "With you, I had a chance at love, at everything I've never known. I kept telling myself I didn't want to hurt you. I didn't, Lara. But this was more about me."

The tightness in his voice twisted her heart. This was a proud man, one who'd restrained his feelings most of his life. She sensed the gift he was really giving her at that moment. "I know." She really understood. He'd been afraid to believe that anyone loved him. He hadn't wanted to be hurt again. Her heart swelling with her love for him and his son, she wished she could ease the moment for him. "I don't give up easily." Needing to touch, she placed her hands on his chest and felt the steady beat of his heart beneath her palm. "I do love you, you know."

He gathered her close to him. "I believe you. I believe I've found someone who means everything to me."

Warm pleasure filled her for what that admittance really meant. He trusted her. She bent her head, blinked away tears.

"Lara, don't," he begged in a whisper. "Don't cry. All I want is to make you happy."

How was it possible she'd been so miserable only

minutes ago? "You already do," she said, caressing his cheek.

Framing her face with his hands, he held it still. "You make me feel—"

"Special," she finished for him. "I hope I make you feel that way." She stared at eyes no longer dull with sadness. "Because you are special to me."

In the slow way she'd always loved, his lips curved up in a smile. "No, it's more than that. You make me believe in something I've never believed in." He fingered a strand of her hair. "I trust you with my son." His eyes held hers. "My heart. And my love. You make me feel whole," he said softly. "I love you, Lara. I love you in a way I never thought was possible."

At last. Tears sprang to her eyes. *He loved her.* Her heart full of joy, she stared up at the balloon. "Is that for real?"

Tenderly he caressed her cheek. "Will you marry me?"

"Yes." She wrapped her arms around his neck. "Oh, yes."

She knew people were around them, didn't care. When he tugged her closer, she tilted up her face to meet his mouth. In his kiss was a message to love her forever. A message filled with all the tenderness and love he'd closed his mind to. She wasn't sure how long they kissed. The sound of clapping drew them apart. Laughing, Lara looked around, saw friends smiling, happy for them. Drawing back, she winked at a beaming Joey. "You know I love your son, don't you?"

Humor danced in his gaze. "Just so you know. He's talking about babies again."

For a second she closed her eyes and gave thanks. All she'd ever wanted was hers. "Maybe someday there'll be more than the three of us." Joy and love bubbled within her. "I should warn you." She couldn't stop smiling. "Twins run in the family."

"The more, the better." Softly he laughed against her cheek. "I like babies."

"I know," she murmured beneath his lips, then kissed him again.

* * * * *

*Be sure to pick up the third book in
Silhouette Special Edition's exciting continuity,*

MANHATTAN MULTIPLES:
HIS PRETEND FIANCÉE

*by Victoria Pade
Available September 2003
Don't miss it!*

Don't miss an exciting new series from

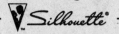

SPECIAL EDITION™

MANHATTAN MULTIPLES
So many babies in the big city!

With five very special love stories:

And Babies Make Four
by MARIE FERRARELLA
Available July 2003 (SE #1551)

The Fertility Factor
by JENNIFER MIKELS
Available August 2003 (SE #1559)

His Pretend Fiancée
by VICTORIA PADE
Available September 2003 (SE #1564)

Practice Makes Pregnant
by LOIS FAYE DYER
Available October 2003 (SE #1569)

Prince of the City
by NIKKI BENJAMIN
Available November 2003 (SE #1575)

Available at your favorite retail outlet.

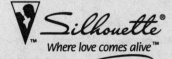

Where love comes alive™

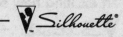

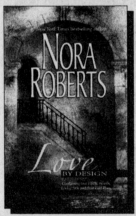

SPECIAL EDITION™

WINCHESTER BRIDES

A WINCHESTER HOMECOMING

Pamela Toth

(Silhouette Special Edition #1562)

Heading home to Colorado to nurse her wounds seemed like a good plan. But the newly divorced Kim Winchester hadn't counted on running headlong into her childhood sweetheart. The one-time rebel has become a seriously handsome rancher—the kind of temptation love-wary Kim would do *anything* to avoid.

Available September 2003 at your favorite retail outlet.

COMING NEXT MONTH

#1561 HARD CHOICES—Allison Leigh
Readers' Ring
A night of passion long ago had resulted in a teenage pregnancy—specifically, the fifteen-year-old who now stood on Annie Hess's doorstep. Now, reformed wild child Annie was forced to confront her past…and Logan Drake, the man who had unknowingly fathered her child.

#1562 A WINCHESTER HOMECOMING—Pamela Toth
Winchester Brides
Kim Winchester returned home after a bitter divorce to find peace—not to face even more emotional turmoil. Seeing rancher and former childhood sweetheart David Major stirred up feelings in her that she'd rather not deal with…feelings that David wouldn't let her ignore.…

#1563 BIG SKY BABY—Judy Duarte
Montana Mavericks: The Kingsleys
Pregnant and alone, Jilly Davis knew there was only one man she could turn to—her best friend, Jeff Forsythe. She needed his strong, dependable shoulder to lean on, but what she found in his arms was an attraction she couldn't deny!

#1564 HIS PRETEND FIANCÉE—Victoria Pade
Manhattan Multiples
Josie Tate was the key to getting firefighter Michael Dunnigan's matchmaking mother off his back. Josie needed a place to stay—and Michael offered his apartment, *if* she would help him make his family believe they were engaged. It seemed like a perfectly practical plan—until Josie's heart got involved.…

#1565 THE BRIDE WORE BLUE JEANS—
Marie Ferrarella
Fiercely independent June Yearling was not looking for love. Her life on the farm was more than enough for her. At least before businessman Kevin Quintano walked into her life… and unleashed a passion she never thought possible!

#1566 FOUR DAYS, FIVE NIGHTS—Christine Flynn
They were stranded in the freezing wilderness and pilot Nick Magruder had to concentrate on getting his passenger, veterinarian Melissa Porter, out alive. He had no time to dwell on her sweet vulnerability—or the softness and heat of her body—as he and Mel huddled together at night.…

SSECNM0803